Ink Inspired

The Beginning to The Montgomery Ink Series

By
Carrie Ann Ryan

Ink Inspired copyright © 2013 Carrie Ann Ryan

All rights reserved.

ISBN-13: 978-1-943123-36-0

Cover Art by Scott Carpenter

This book is a work of fiction. The names, characters, places, and incidents are products of the author's imagination or have been used fictitiously and are not to be construed as real. Any resemblance to persons, living or dead, actual events, locals or organizations is entirely coincidental. All rights reserved. With the exception of quotes used in reviews, this book may not be reproduced or used in whole or in part by any means existing without written permission from the author

Ink Inspired

Shepard Montgomery loves the feel of a needle in his hands, the ink that he lays on another, and the thrill he gets when his art is finished, appreciated, and loved. At least that's the way it used to be. Now he's struggling to figure out why he's a tattoo artist at all as he wades through the college frat boys and tourists who just want a thrill, not a permanent reminder of their trip. Once he sees the Ice Princess walk through Midnight Ink's doors though, he knows he might just have found the inspiration he needs.

Shea Little has spent her life listening to her family's desires. She went to the best schools, participated in the most proper of social events, and almost married the man her family wanted for her. When she ran from that and found a job she actually likes, she thought she'd rebelled enough. Now though, she wants one more thing—only Shepard stands in the way. She'll not only have to let him learn more about her in order to get inked, but find out what it means to be truly free.

CHAPTER ONE

"Can you make her boobs bigger?"

Shepard Montgomery raised a brow but didn't say anything. Honestly, there really wasn't anything he *could* say at the moment without laughing.

Or knocking the dude out cold.

"No, really. I want her boobs, like, enormous. Way bigger than Justin's."

Shep blinked.

"Justin's?" he drawled, his voice gruff. Seriously, this kid was going to kill him.

The client snorted. "Oh, you know what I mean. Justin. My friend? The chick he has inked on his back has big boobs. I want mine bigger."

Shep closed his eyes, trying to think of a delicate way to put the fact that, no, he did not want to ink this virgin with a big-breasted woman just because the dude wanted to show up his bro. Oh, and the other dude was totally a bro in every sense of the word. These two noobs had to be the most ignorant college pricks to ever walk in this shop demanding Shep ink them with whatever shit they wanted. Sure, he hadn't inked Justin, but still...they didn't even care that they would have to live the rest of their lives with shit ink—not that Shep gave shit ink—because they were fucking idiots.

He should just tell this prick to fuck himself, but this was his job. He probably shouldn't be so honest.

No, wait, he didn't actually care what this dude thought of him.

It wasn't as if he was *trying* to be the best customer service rep in the biz.

Oh no, he didn't give a fuck.

"No, kid, I'm not inking you with a big-breasted woman just because you want to show up your bro."

The kid's eyes widened then narrowed in that annoying rich-kid-on-daddy's-dime sort of way.

"Hey, I pay for it. You do it, bro. I don't see the fucking problem. I just want a chick with big tits on my back. Bigger tits than Justin's bitch."

Shep slowly put down the pen he'd been about to take notes with and scooted his stool back. His six-five frame didn't make it comfortable, but he didn't give a shit at the moment.

"Okay, *bro*, this is how it's gonna go. You ain't getting a tat here. Not now. Maybe not ever. You think money gives you the right to come into the best shop in New Orleans and boss us around like you fucking own the place?"

"It's your *job*," the little prick spat.

"No. It's my job to ink art on canvas. That canvas just happens to be skin. Today, though? No fucking way. Not on you. You're welcome to come back when you got a fucking clue what you want to ink on yourself, but fuck right now, dude. You want some strange woman's face, some generic shit on your back? It's not even a sexy old-school pinup. No. That's not how it's done. You want bigger tits on the woman because you want to one-up your bro? Dude, if you ain't got the bigger dick, that ink ain't gonna help."

The kid blinked, the slow crawl of crimson staining his cheeks either from anger or embarrassment—probably a mix of both—making him look even younger than nineteen.

"You should get a tat that means something to you, or at least isn't a fucking joke. You don't come in here waving your dick and ordering me around."

"Hey!"

"Oh, and another thing. You ever, *ever*, fucking call a woman—*any* woman—a bitch again, I'll knock that little smirk right off your fucking face. Get out of my chair. You're done."

"Fuck you! I'll go get my tat from a place that actually treats their customers like they're supposed to. Not from some washed-out, has-been artist who doesn't know shit."

The kid stomped out, every eye on the place following him.

Shep closed his eyes and prayed for peace.

Fuck.

He was thirty-eight years old, and this was what his life had come to.

Douchebag college boys who wanted big boobs.

Great.

"Smooth, dude. Why don't you just kick the puppy next time? Make it easier," Sassy, Midnight Ink's receptionist and all-around crazy person, sing-songed as she walked past him.

"Shut up, Sass, please. I'm not in the mood."

"You never are anymore, baby. That's the problem. Though, honestly, I have no idea why you said yes to that little prick for a consultation in the first place. You could tell from just looking at him he'd be a B-back."

A B-back was a dude who said they'd be right back after they went to the ATM or gave some other lame excuse, saying they'd 'be back' only they'd chicken out and never come back.

Yeah, the kid looked like he'd be one, though if he'd wanted to impress his friends enough, maybe not.

"Sass, really? I'm not in the mood," he grumbled as he cleaned his station. He hadn't had a client yet that morning, but he wanted no trace of that *bro* near his place.

"You should have let Caliph take it," Sass said, an annoyingly bright grin on her face.

Midnight Ink, their shop right on Canal Street, had several artists who worked in shifts. They didn't have to come in every day, only if they wanted to get paid. Since everyone working there needed money to pay for shit, they all came in. Most worked on walk-ins around their scheduled clients, but a few took on only clients they'd hand-picked off the waiting lists. Those guys also only did ink with certain elements because they were the *shit* at it.

Shep did a bit of everything, so, even though his shading was fucking awesome, he didn't specialize too much. His best friend, Caliph, was the same way.

Shep would have given his left nut to see his brick house of a best friend take on that college kid.

"What's this I hear about me taking on a bro?" Caliph asked, stomping through the room to his station.

Shep was big.

Caliph was bigger.

And scarier.

"Had a perfect kid for you," Shep yelled across the shop, causing a few of the customers to turn toward him. "Wanted big tits like his bro."

Caliph snorted, then flipped him off. "Fuck off, Shep."

Ah, a decade of friendship never lost its shine.

Shep shook his head then gave Sassy and Caliph a chin nod to say he was going out for a coffee. Sassy might make some of the best brew right in their shop, but he didn't want to sit there too long. He needed space.

Again.

He needed to think, and the muggy air of New Orleans always

did it for him. Sure, it wasn't the crisp, clean air of the Rocky Mountains where he'd grown up, but he liked it. His family—who all still lived up near Denver—thought he was fucking nuts for moving down to New Orleans to set up shop, or at least find a shop he could fit into, but he loved it.

Well, at least he used to.

Fuck, he needed to get his head out of his ass and figure out what was wrong with his mood. He was thirty-eight, not some young kid, but sure as hell not on his way out. Maybe he needed a change.

He just had no idea what kind of change.

Shep turned the corner to make his way to the coffee shop then cursed as a little bit of a thing ran straight into him.

He sucked in a breath as she looked up at him—way up at him.

Damn, her eyes were something else. A pale, pale blue that looked almost like crystals in water on a sunny day.

Those had to be fucking contacts because no way were those eyes real.

"I'm so sorry, sir. I wasn't watching where I was going. Excuse me." The little blonde thing walked around him after she mumbled her apologies heading the other direction.

Shep blinked.

Well, hell. That was weird. He hadn't even had a chance to say anything—something like "fucking sexy eyes" or anything along those lines that could have made her want join him for coffee.

Shep shook his head. Fuck, he needed that coffee. In the long scheme of things, what he didn't need was a wide-eyed woman who probably thought he looked like some ex-con with his full sleeves and the scar on his brow, not to mention the other piercings and tats hidden from view.

No, he didn't need that shit.

What he did need? Well, that was the problem.

He didn't know.

He ordered a coffee from the girl at the counter, who fluttered her lashes at him. Shep held back a groan—and not the good kind. This kid had to be in her early twenties, if that. There was no way Shep would cross that boundary, even if she was hot as hell, which she was.

He walked to one of the tables outside the café and sat down with his cup, not ready to go back to work yet. Fuck, if he was thinking some twenty-something was hot, maybe he just needed to get laid. That might be the answer to all his problems, though even a long night of against-the-wall sex might not be enough to get him out of his funk. The fact that he'd blown up at a silly kid just now told him something was far from good.

He needed to figure out what the hell was going on with him, find his path, find his inspiration.

And fast.

Shep took a deep breath of humid New Orleans air then a sip of his coffee. Damn, he loved the coffee down here. Nothing bitter or over-brewed about it. Sure, when he went up north to Denver to visit his folks he didn't mind the little cafés, but to Shep, nothing was better than New Orleans coffee.

Since they were in the Deep South, it didn't really feel as though they'd just hit the start of January. The holidays seemed like something in the distant past, and the New Year's parties—

something New Orleans did fucking right every time—were a fading memory.

What wasn't a memory was his resolution.

Nope. The fact that he'd told himself *this* year would be different wasn't lost on him. He'd resolved to find his inspiration and actually do art that meant something to both him and the client rather than just walk-in after walk-in.

Shep ran a hand over his five-day-old beard and sighed.

When the fuck had he turned into some emo teen?

His phone buzzed in his pocket, and he pulled it out of his jeans. When he saw his cousin Austin's name on the screen, he smiled. If anyone could get him out of his funk, it was Austin.

"Hey, what's up?"

"Nothing," Austin said, his voice even deeper than Shep's.

"Just got done with a whole back piece that took six sittings. Now I'm trying to get my head out of phoenix feathers and into dragon scales."

"Did you take a pic?"

"Sure as fuck did." Austin laughed. "I'll text it to you in a bit. Fine piece of work if I do say so myself. I was bored and didn't feel like walking anywhere to grab a bite. Figured I'd call and see how you're doing. We didn't get to talk much when you were up for Christmas."

Almost the entire Montgomery clan lived up in the Denver area. Shep was one of the few who had ventured out. Though he and Austin were the closest and the same age, when Shep had gone up for the holidays, he didn't have that much time for his favorite cousin. Oh no. Between Austin's seven siblings, Shep's three siblings, the other Montgomery cousins, plus all the aunts, uncles, and parents, the holidays were a bitch, giving him no time to breathe.

"Yeah, it sucked that we couldn't get together much when I was up there. You should come down here for a visit. Come see the color and culture. Put it in your ink."

Austin and his sister Maya owned Montgomery Ink, a shop in Denver and were hella good at what they did. The three of them frequently went around the country to see what inspiration they could find and what they could translate into their work.

Maybe he needed to do that again and find that *thing* he was looking for.

Whatever the hell that *thing* was.

"Maybe," Austin hedged, causing Shep to frown. "We'll see."

"What's up, man?"

"Nothing. Just getting old."

Shep snorted. "Tell me about it. We're the same age, remember? What's going on?"

Austin sighed. "Fuck it. I'll come down there. Leave Maya alone with the shop for a bit. God knows she likes to be by herself with the place most days."

Shep smiled at Austin's description of Maya. Fuck knew Austin was right.

"I'm here when you come down. You know I have the guest room you can bunk in. We're not kids anymore where you have to find a futon or couch."

"Thank God for that. Thanks, man."

Shep smiled. "You're welcome. I think we're just hitting the age where we're too old to figure out what the hell we want but know we need to find it someway."

INK INSPIRED

"Maybe, Shep. Maybe."

They said their goodbyes, and Shep ended the call, feeling a bit better that his cousin was coming down soon. They'd finalize plans later since Austin would have to talk to Maya before traveling. There was no way they'd cross that woman and her sharp tongue.

Shep finished his coffee and headed back to Midnight Ink. He needed to get some work done. He might not have an appointment that day—something rare for him, thankfully—but there were bound to be walk-ins.

As soon as he stepped inside, he spotted her.

That sexy fairy who'd walked into him on the street.

Her blonde hair was even lighter than he'd thought considering they'd been out in the sunlight before. No, that hadn't been the sun making her look gorgeous.

That was all her.

She wore a light gray pencil skirt with a light pink top and gray jacket. Her heels were demure, but fuck, they made her legs look sexy

She looked like someone's assistant or an accountant.

Totally out of place in a tattoo shop, at least in most shops.

Midnight Ink didn't discriminate. They knew some people had to hide their ink because of work so they made sure it looked hella good underneath their clothes.

This woman though?

Totally out of place.

And lost.

Shep smiled.

He could totally help her with that.

Sassy stood by the woman, her brow raised. "Honey, you

sure you want this one? I know you were looking at something else a minute ago."

The woman turned and bit her lip, forcing Shep to hold back a groan.

Holy fuck. He was acting like some teenager with a hard-on, rather than a not-so-young man with a hard-on.

Sassy spotted him and waved him over. "Here's Shep, honey. He'll be the one to ink you since he has time and you said it didn't matter who did it. Shep, this is Shea. She's all yours." Sassy raised that brow again and Shep smiled.

Oh, yes. He wanted to get his hands on this woman in every way possible.

Ink would be just the first step.

The woman turned toward him, and Shep bit back a curse.

Fuck.

That wasn't just indecision in her eyes. That was pure fear mixed with something else. Something like determination.

The kind of determination that led to inked regrets.

Sassy walked away, leaving Shep and Shea alone in the corner, a stack of albums between them.

"So, uh, Shep," she started, her voice just as smooth and sexy as it had been outside. "Sorry again for walking into you earlier."

"Like I said, it's no problem."

"So, uh, I guess you'll be giving me my tattoo? I think I want this little daisy. Or maybe this butterfly. Can you do that?"

Shep looked down her body, her out-of-place clothes, the fear sliding right off her, and her weight shifting from foot to foot. He raised his gaze and met her eyes.

INK INSPIRED

"No."

CHAPTER TWO

"No?" Shea Little squeaked.

"No," the very sexy tattoo artist, Shep, repeated. He folded his arms—his *very* sexy, tattooed, muscled arms—over his chest, and she blinked. A lock of dark hair fell over his eyes, making him look even more dangerous—and even a little dashing.

Oh great, now she made him sound like a romantic rake.

Not the man telling her no.

"But...why? Just no?" She couldn't understand what he was saying. She'd come in to Midnight Ink after talking herself in and out of doing this for two straight weeks, and the first artist she'd spoken to said no?

That made absolutely no sense to her.

Shep raised a brow. "Tell me why you want a tattoo." His forearms flexed, and she pulled herself away from the tantalizing sight.

"Why?" she croaked, annoyed with herself for sounding like an idiot.

She normally didn't have an issue speaking intelligently, but apparently standing in front of a way-too-attractive man, along with her frayed nerves for even *thinking* about getting a tattoo, was too much for her.

"Yes, why. Why do you want a tattoo? You stick out like a sore thumb, babe. Not that that's an issue usually, but right here, right now? You should tell me why you want it. Is this just a sudden urge to show off your bad-girl side? Or do you have more ink under those prim and proper clothes of yours? I'm guessing not, considering you look like you're freaked the fuck out by just being here."

"I'm not freaked out," she lied.

Oh, she was definitely freaked out.

This...this *man,* though, didn't have to be so rude and call her out on it. She'd already spent all morning pacing her apartment trying to figure out how to gain the courage to even come into the shop. Now this man wanted to know why she wanted a tattoo when even she didn't even know the answer.

Plus, she was pretty sure he'd just insulted her looks—or at least what she was wearing.

Sure, she knew her normal attire didn't fit in with what the clientele of this establishment usually wore, but he didn't have to point it out.

God, he was infuriating, and she hadn't even spoken with him using complete sentences. Not logical ones anyway.

Shea forced her gaze from his strong build and the tattoos that covered his arms and peeked out over his collar, and looked around at the shop. She was pretty sure every set of eyes was focused on them. Some looked intrigued, some bored, others openly gaped at the spectacle of she and Shep arguing.

Well, *him* arguing.

She hadn't exactly stood up for herself yet, something she knew she needed to do one way or another. It was about time she did so. After all, the whole idea of getting a tattoo was to prove to herself she could be assertive.

There.

That was it.

That was what she'd tell this Shep with the dreamy blue eyes, not that he deserved an explanation since he was acting like a butt.

"Shea?" Shep asked, and she froze at the sound of her name coming from his lips.

Oh, yes, she liked that a lot.

Way too much, in fact, considering she didn't know him, and from what she'd seen, she wasn't sure she even *wanted* to know him. He was an egotistical asshole for sure and not someone she *needed* to get to know.

She'd just have to ask that receptionist with the pretty pink streak in her hair. Sassy. Yes, that was her name. Sassy seemed as though she'd be able to help her.

"What?" she snapped, the anger lying under the surface finally threatening to break free.

Something flashed in his eyes, and he grinned.

Darn it, the man looked hot when he did that.

And he had a dimple.

Great.

"Why do you want a tattoo, Shea?" he asked softly.

His tone got under her skin this time. Or at least it did in a whole new way. He seemed as though he genuinely wanted to know, rather than asking just to be a prick about it.

At least that's what she hoped she got from his voice.

Knowing her luck, she was totally wrong and he was actually a jerk.

"Why do you need to know?" she asked, almost unable to get the words out. She was losing her nerve, and she knew it. She shouldn't have come. She pulled her purse tighter to her body and lifted her chin. She'd just have to leave the shop.

There wouldn't be a second chance for her. She'd been an idiot for even considering coming here and doing something so radical for her.

Her mother and ex were right. She was a stiff, cold mannequin.

Totally not appropriate for a man like Shep.

She swallowed.

Jesus. Why was she even thinking about this man? This was about a *tattoo*, and she wasn't getting one. Shep had nothing to do with any of it.

Nothing.

"Sorry to have bothered you and taken your time." She pulled her purse closer to her and walked quickly toward the door, her high heels clicking on the smooth wood floor. It took all she had to hold back the tears and keep her body from shaking.

She knew her face had to be red, but she ignored it.

This had been a stupid, stupid idea.

A large, warm hand gripped her elbow as she reached the sidewalk, and she tried to pull away.

"Wait, Shea, don't go."

"Unhand me," she spat through clenched teeth. "Don't touch me."

Please don't touch me.

He didn't let go but pulled her toward him so they were

facing each other. Sweat dripped down her silk-covered back, and she tilted her head so she could look at his bearded face as the cloying New Orleans heat surrounded them.

Shea could hear the hustle and bustle of tourists and locals, either working or sightseeing. She could hear children laughing, couples talking, a lone man humming, another yelling on his phone. Yet all of that became background noise and paled in comparison to those pretty blue eyes rimmed in dark lashes and against striking cheekbones beneath a few days' worth of beard.

Shep finally pulled back but was close enough to her that she couldn't move away and run like she wanted to. Damn it. She hated not being in control, not having all the answers and everything in its place. Yes, this

She raised her chin. "That may be, but I'm not in need of *ink* anymore. I made a mistake. Goodbye, Shep."

She turned, but he caught her elbow again. "Jesus, Shea, you put up that ice princess mask quickly, but hell, I saw the fear in your eyes when I walked up to you. Plus I saw it when we bumped into each other on the street before I even knew you were coming to Midnight for a tattoo. Tell me what's going on in that mind of yours."

He reached up and tucked a lock of hair behind her ear, and she froze. The gesture was so intimate, so close, that she wasn't sure what to do. She didn't even know this man, and he was touching her, making her want to know about his own ink.

There had to be something wrong with her.

"I...I...why are you doing that?"

"Doing what?" he asked, his voice low.

Jesus, his voice was sexy. It had a low, throaty sound that rumbled against her skin, forcing her to hold back a shiver. She thought only sexy guys on TV or in the movies had voices like that.

"Why are you touching me? I told you not to touch me." Her voice had risen at the end of that, her fear of something...new coming out.

"I'm an artist, Shea, not a mind reader."

She blinked. "What?"

"I'm an artist. I fucking love what I do." He stopped and shook his head, this time a little doubt entering his eyes that confused her. "Well, I've always loved what I do. I've been in a little rough patch lately, like I need to find my muse or whatever."

Shea snorted. "Seriously? Does that line work on anyone? No. Don't even bother answering. I've already told you I was sorry for taking your time, and now you're taking mine. Just let me leave, and I will be on my way. Soon I won't even be a memory for you, and you can use that muse line on some unsuspecting coed."

Shep threw his head back and laughed. It had to be wrong that she loved the way his throat worked as he did so.

Yeah, she totally had issues.

"Honey, I'm way too fucking old to be looking at some coed, and that wasn't a line, the thing about the muse. I've been in a funk, and that has nothing to do with getting laid or even working on your ink. And I do, by the way, want to work your ink. When I saw you on the street a little while ago I was intrigued. That doesn't happen often. Not anymore. So, yeah, I want to see what tattoo you want and why. I want to get to know you."

That threw her. Get to know her? Just what exactly was he saying? And now he wanted to ink her? This Shep was making her head spin in more ways than one.

"You're going to have to take this one step at a time for me, Shep," she finally said after she took a deep breath to gather her thoughts. "One minute you're acting like a brute, telling me I can't have a tattoo and I stick out like a sore thumb. You say you aren't hitting on me, but you're intrigued and want to work on my *ink,* as you put it."

Shep smiled, a flash of white against his beard. "Sounds about right."

"You make no sense. I'm just going to go." She was done. She had been an idiot to even think about coming down to Midnight. Though this hadn't been an impulsive decision—not by far— she still felt out of her depths. That feeling wasn't something she enjoyed, and giving up at this point seemed like the best option.

"Don't go, Shea."

She hated how much she loved the sound of her name on his lips.

"Why should I stay?"

"Because you came here for a reason. I don't know what it is yet, considering I'm still waiting for that answer to my first question. You should also stay because, despite the clothes you're wearing, the ice you've shielded yourself with, and the fear in your eyes, you still had the balls to walk through those doors. Now, don't get me wrong, we're not that scary in there. Okay, maybe Caliph is, but other than that, we're good. We wouldn't hurt you, and we're not the scary deviants you might think we are from watching movies or some shit."

Shea had no idea who Caliph was, but she knew the people in that building weren't too scary. She didn't judge people on their appearances like so many others did, like so many judged her.

"I need to go," she whispered, scared now for a whole other reason.

"Tell me why you want a tattoo."

She huffed out a breath and looked into his eyes. "I want one because…because it's not me. Or at least not the me everyone else thinks I am. I'm tired, Shep. So, so tired of being…this." She pointed down at herself and sighed.

He cupped her face, and she gasped, unprepared for his

heated touch. "That's all I wanted to hear, Shea. Now, what do you want?"

You.

She blinked. Well, that stray thought was just freaking crazy. She didn't even know him.

"I don't know," she answered honestly. "I want something that's me. I just don't know what or who that is."

Shep pulled away slightly, and she felt the loss of his touch down to her bones. "Okay then. I'll help you. Whatever you want, it should be something that's just for you, a design that makes doing something different worth it." He grinned. "Plus, in order to find out what will work for you, I get the opportunity to know you better. A definite plus for me."

He wanted to get to know her? Her? The ice princess in pale clothes who liked to blend into the woodwork if she could?

"Do you always get so personal with your clients?" she asked, a strange line of jealousy threading its way through her. She didn't want to be just another woman he *got to know* before he inked her and left.

Well, hell, now she sounded crazy.

He brushed her cheek with the tip of his finger, and she held back a shudder. "I've never done it like this before," he said softly. "I'm marking someone's skin forever. It's always personal. It doesn't matter if I don't know everything about them or what makes them tick. I do know what that tattoo means to them—at least a semblance of it. I can't just sit back and watch you make a decision you might regret."

"You don't know me well enough to know I'll regret it." No one did.

"I want to know you enough."

She'd come to Midnight Ink for a reason, and now Shep was going to help her. No matter that she thought she was crazy and everyone who knew her would think the same, there was only one answer.

"Yes. Okay. Let's do that."

Shep grinned and leaned forward. Shea's chin raised on its own accord, but he didn't kiss her. She felt oddly bereft that he didn't even try, but she didn't say anything. He brushed her cheek once more and smiled softly.

He reached around to his back pocket and pulled out a card. "Here you go. Take this and I'll get yours."

She nodded and pulled a card out of her purse. He looked down and smiled. "Accountant. Totally knew it."

Great. She even *looked* boring.

INK INSPIRED

"Hey now. I like prim and proper. I'll call you in a bit, and we can talk about what we're going to do and how I'm going to help you find the perfect ink."

"Okay," she whispered, not feeling at all like the cold woman she usually was. Shep seemed to heat her up from the inside out, and she wasn't sure how she felt about that.

With one last look, he walked back into Midnight, leaving her on the street, dazed. She shook her head, made her way back to her car, then back to her house, his card still clutched in her palm. She never took days off, but she'd taken this one off to get it done and now the day was ruined, wasted.

She had no idea what she was doing.

Shea walked into her home and took a look around. The prim house, the prim decorations, the prim...everything. None of it showcased who she was.

No, it told her who her mother was and what her mother wanted for her when Shea bought the house. Shea had long ago given up the fight when it came to what her mother wanted.

Well, other than leaving Richard, her ex-fiancé. Her mother had screamed and threatened to disown her for making what she considered the mistake of a lifetime.

Shea never could live up to her mother's dreams.

She took off her shoes and walked to the couch, sinking into its cushions. Everything around her was so cold, uninviting, but the cushions on the couch were soft enough that she could at least get somewhat comfortable.

The card in her hand called to her, and she looked down at it. What the heck was she doing?

She had gone into Midnight Ink because her New Year's resolution was to do something for herself, something so out of character that she just might be able to find the person she wanted to be.

She'd always loved ink. She loved the way people looked with it. She thought the swirls, dark colors, and shading were freaking sexy. She'd always been too chicken to do anything about it before. Now, though, she wanted it.

She just didn't have a clue about what design she wanted. Shep was going to help with that though.

Shep.

His dark hair and light eyes called to her, even if she had no idea why. He was going to help her find herself. Okay, that sounded lame, even though it was true.

Everything could go up in flames if she made the wrong choice, but it didn't matter.

It was all or nothing.

Her cell rang, and she frowned. God, she hoped it wasn't Richard or her mother. They never stopped bugging her with their own opinions on how she should run her life.

She didn't recognize the number on the screen, so she answered as coolly as possible.

"Yes?"

"Shea? It's Shep."

Her pulse beat in her ears, and she swallowed hard.

"Yes, this is Shea."

"I'm glad you didn't give me a fake card. That's why I asked for that rather than you putting your number in my phone. Harder to fake that on the fly."

"Oh. I guess."

Great. She needed to learn to use complete sentences, or he was going to think she was a complete idiot.

"What do you say I take you out for a night on the town tomorrow night after my shift?"

"Why? For what?"

He gave a deep chuckle, and it shot straight between her legs. Dear Lord, even the man's laugh was sexy.

"I told you I want to get to know you to help you. And fuck, just to get to know *you*. I'm thinking we can pick up a quick dinner then spend the rest of the night exploring to see what you like. What do you say?"

He wanted to do something without a firm schedule she could check over and over again? She wasn't a hundred percent sure of that; this wasn't normal for her. She didn't *want* it to be normal.

"Okay. That sounds fine."

"Good. I'll meet you in front of the shop at seven tomorrow.

That way you'll feel more comfortable than me coming to your house and freaking you out."

She relaxed and smiled, even though he couldn't see it. She didn't know how he knew she was worried about him knowing where she lived, but she liked it.

"Okay."

"Okay then. See you tomorrow, Shea."

"Tomorrow, Shep."

He hung up, and she stared at the phone, not sure what had just happened. She'd spent too much of her life on the sidelines, and this man and his ideas could help her.

Those striking blue eyes, the scratchy voice, and his sexy tattoos just might be worth upsetting her whole world order.

CHAPTER THREE

Shep changed needles, finished with the overall outline and ready for shading. He rolled his shoulders and took a look at his work.

Not bad.

Okay, it was better than that. Way fucking better, but he knew it was a process, and he was never happy with his work until the finished project. Each layer of outlining, shading, and color added to the overall look. He knew what he wanted and how that blended with what the client wanted. Eventually, once he added the final layers, the tat would look fucking amazing. Now, though, it was only a half-finished piece.

"How's it looking?" the man on the bench asked, careful not to turn around.

Shep was in the middle of putting a kick-ass phoenix on the man's back with its wings wrapping around the side. He'd finished the outline in their last session and was going over certain spots today to make sure they were perfect. Then he'd be doing some of the initial shading before he added color. He usually waited to do the shading, but he wanted to make sure it didn't look too dark since the vibrant orange and reds really needed to pop in the finished piece.

"It's gonna fucking rock," Shep answered and began the shading. The buzzing sound of the needle shot straight through him as it always did. He loved shading the best because the needle moved at a slower pace, and for most people, it felt hella good.

From the way his client moaned, Shep wasn't wrong.

He worked for another two hours, his mind on his hands and his ink. While some people might daydream while working, his job was a little different. One wrong movement and he'd fuck up someone's skin.

Not cool.

Even as he tried to keep focus, though, his thoughts went to the woman with pale, pale blue eyes...like crystals in water on a sunny day and a pixie face.

Shea.

Jesus, he liked that smooth-as-silk yet hard-as-ice woman, and he didn't even know her past a few words and touches.

There had to be something wrong with him. He'd never been drawn to a woman like her at all.

Shep moved back and shook his head while cleaning off the leftover ink, plasma, and blood from where he was working. He seriously needed to get his mind off Shea and their date tonight. She might not call it a date, but he would. He wanted her, and he wasn't going to lie to himself about it. He was way too damned old for that.

He rolled his shoulders and got back to work. This phoenix was going to fucking rock. He'd known it when he'd first done the sketches over a month ago, but it wasn't until now that he really thought it could be something big.

There was another spark running along his skin, getting him excited about what he was doing for the first time in way too long.

It had to be Shea. She was the only thing different in his life, even though she really wasn't a huge part of it.

At least not yet.

He was going to change that.

He grinned and started on some of the color for the wings, getting into each stroke of the needle.

After another hour and a half, he pulled back, sweat marking his brow and his back straining. Too many hours bent over a table would do that to a man.

He snorted, thinking about what Caliph or Austin would say to him if he'd said that aloud.

Yeah, not sharing that thought.

He cleaned up the guy's back then put ointment on the area. "Okay, you're all done for this session. I think one more should do it."

The guy got up and smiled. "You're a god with the needle, Shep. It didn't hurt a bit."

Shep grinned. "Even if it did, you'd like it."

He threw his head back and laughed. "True. So when can we do our last session?"

Shep went through the aftercare instructions. This guy was a regular, but it never hurt to go over them again. The last thing Shep wanted was a shitty healing and cleanup job to ruin his art. They scheduled the session for three weeks from then when they both had time, and Shep went back to clean up his space.

He'd really gotten into the piece, and it had taken a full hour longer than he'd intended. It was already quarter 'til seven. He wouldn't have time to head home and grab a quick shower.

Shit.

He hadn't wanted to look like a sweaty loser for his date, but she'd have to take what she got. After all, he was just Shep. He'd have to be good enough.

He went to the employee restroom and stripped off his shirt, then pulled another on. He would still wear his worn-in jeans and boots, but at least he had a black button-down to wear. It was just getting to that time of year when it was muggy at night too, so he didn't bother with his leather jacket. He ran his hand through his hair and called it a day.

He didn't look like some *GQ* model with the tats, nipple

piercings—and more—but he did all right for himself. From the way Shea's gaze raked his body the day before, he had a feeling what he had did it for her. What she had sure as fuck did it for him.

"Looking good," Sassy said as she walked to the back to get her purse. "Though you might have wanted to shower before your big date with the ice princess."

He scowled. "Don't call her that. And how the hell do you know I have a date tonight with her?"

"Sassy knows all."

Shep rolled his eyes. "You were lurking around the corner when I called her yesterday, weren't you?"

She just raised her brow. "I have no idea what you are talking about. Sassy doesn't lurk."

"Stop talking about yourself in third person. You're creeping me out."

She just shook her head and laughed. "Spray yourself down with some cologne but not that frat-boy crap with the shitty commercials."

"I don't even own the frat-boy crap, Sass."

"Then we won't have a problem. Good luck with your main squeeze tonight, sugar. You're gonna need it."

"What the fuck do you mean by that? You saying I'm not good enough for her?"

She held her palms out. "That's not what I'm saying at all. I'm just saying that woman had a shield around her so tight that even I couldn't see through, and you know I'm good as fuck when it comes to that. You'll have to break through that ice if you want to know who she is. And what the fuck is with you saying you're not good enough? You've never been one to lack self-esteem, Shep. What's going on?"

Shep shook his head. "Never mind. I'm just antsy."

Sassy smiled and twirled the long strip of pink hair between her fingers. "I see. So this one's special. Good to know."

Shep narrowed his eyes. "Back off, Sassy."

"Don't worry, sugar. I'm sure everything will work out." With that, she sauntered out of the room, hips swaying.

Jesus, that woman was a nut job sometimes.

Shea would be outside within the next five minutes, and he didn't want her to wait. Remembering the way she'd looked like a frightened rabbit the last time he'd seen her, he wasn't about to leave it up to fate that she'd actually stay.

His phone buzzed against his leg, and he cursed. It better not be Shea calling to cancel.

Without looking at the screen, he answered. "You better be outside and not ready to cancel on me, babe."

"Having to threaten your dates now? What the hell is going on in New Orleans that a Montgomery is losing their street cred?"

Shep cursed at Austin's words. "Jesus. I thought you were someone else."

"Clearly. What's wrong? Having trouble in the sack?"

"I'm not talking about sex with you, Austin, just because you aren't getting any. I don't have time to discuss it right now."

"Ouch. Cruel words for a man who thinks his date is about to dump him."

"Shut it. I've got to go since Shea is probably outside waiting for me and I'm here talking with you."

"Shea, is it? Pretty name."

"Austin," Shep growled.

"Hey, don't jump on me. Go on your date if she shows. Hope she does because I'm not in the mood to deal with your emo bullshit if she doesn't. I called to tell you I booked a flight to come down there in three days. That cool?"

Shep sighed. He knew Austin needed to come down and clear his head for whatever reason, and Shep wanted to help. Even though they got on each other's nerves, they were family.

"Yeah, man. It's cool."

"Good. And, Shep? For what it's worth, I hope she shows. Just the way you said her name made me think she's something."

He hung up, leaving Shep staring at his phone. Jesus. Did he have a sign around his neck saying that Shea was different? He hadn't even really told himself that, and yet everyone seemed to know.

He just hoped he didn't scare her off.

Shep made his way through the front door and froze.

Holy fuck.

Shea was even sexier than he remembered, and he remembered every detail about her from the day before.

She wore a white dress with one of those cuts that went right across the shoulders but still showed some skin and made her look hella tantalizing. She had on a light pink cardigan that covered most of her arms and pearls.

Fucking *pearls*.

Not too big, but Jesus, she was classy.

Her dress was tight at her waist and hips and flared out at her knees. Her legs looked fucking delicious in high-heeled pink pumps with skinny little heels.

She'd put her hair in a bun at the nape of her neck so he could see all the contours of her face. Though she wasn't all bones and angles, her cheekbones were sharp and made those hypnotic eyes pop.

Right now, though, those eyes were full of fear…and excitement.

He could work with the latter.

And he'd have to get rid of the former.

She stared up at him, a small, strained smile on her face, and he took a deep breath, forcing himself back so he wouldn't jump on her like a frat boy in public.

"Shea, you made it."

She blinked up at him, her gaze moving from his chest to his face.

Nice.

"I told you I'd be here. I don't back away from my engagements." She blushed. "Except for when I'm cornered and not wanted. Then I leave. I mean…"

He took two steps toward her and cupped her face. "Breathe, Shea. I know I freaked you out yesterday. Let's go have fun, shall we? Let loose a bit?"

She snorted. "I'm not one to let loose."

Oh, he'd figured that, though the fact she'd come into Midnight Ink in the first place told him she was beyond ready to do just that. She might wear the clothes of an ice princess, but he had a feeling she was hot as hell underneath them.

It was his goal to find out.

And not just for heat.

Oh no.

He wanted more.

"You'll have fun tonight. I promise." He moved to pull her closer, wrapping his arm around her shoulders. She stiffened for a moment then relaxed a bit against him.

Progress.

"I have no idea why I'm doing this, but the heck with it. I'm doing it." She looked up at him from beneath her lashes. "So, what exactly is it I'm doing?"

He grinned down at her and kissed her nose, unable to stop himself. She jerked back slightly, a blush rising in her cheeks, but she didn't call him out on it.

"We're going to Frenchman Street."

"The street? Not a specific place?"

"You've been down there before?"

She nodded. "A couple of times. It's very…colorful."

"Tactful, baby. It's not the main tourist destination and doesn't have the most famous places and foodie type things, but it has great fucking music in the bars and even right on the streets. It's just about getting to the time where people will be doing pub crawls and enjoying themselves. We'll blend in and find out if you like it." He looked down at her dress and pumps. "Well, we'll try to blend it. You'll look like a tourist, but I'll take care of you."

She stopped, her face blushing. "Oh crap. I'm sorry. I didn't know where we were going, so I just put this on. I can go back and change. Shep, darn it, I don't know what I'm doing."

He turned her in his arms and crushed his lips to hers. She sucked in a breath, her lips parting. His tongue bushed against hers, and he lost himself, inhaling her scent, tasting it, savoring it.

He pulled back, out of breath. "Calm down, baby. It's okay. Dress the way you want to dress. I won't judge. Just don't hide yourself. Got it?"

"You...you kissed me."

"Fuck yeah. It was perfect."

She touched her swollen lips with her fingertips, her gaze dazed. "Oh...my." She blinked. "Next time give me an idea of where we're going, and I'll dress better, okay? I hate standing out. I just put on something cute for the night. I wasn't thinking."

He nodded, loving the fact she'd said next time because, fuck yeah, there'd be a next time. "You pulled off cute and then some, Shea. I'll warn you what we're doing next time, though. You'll always stand out to me though, baby. Got that?"

She tilted her head. "I'm not sure that I do." She held up her hand. "Don't explain it. Everything is going a little too fast for me right now, so let it go. I'll dress differently next time, and we'll be okay."

He smiled, nodding. "You going to be okay in those fuck-me pumps?"

She looked down at her feet then looked up at him, her gaze wide. "Fuck-me pumps?" she blurted. "These aren't black, and I could have added another inch and been fine. Oh no, Shep. These totally aren't fuck-me pumps."

Shep had to swallow hard at the thought of her in taller heels.

In nothing but those heels.

Holy. Fuck.

"Okay then, babe. You told me. Let me know if your feet hurt though. I'll take care of you."

She smiled and his heart lurched. Fuck, he was in trouble.

"I'll be fine, Shep. I love heels. But thank you for thinking of me."

They made their way to Frenchman Street, not talking much on their way. Sure, he wanted to get to know her, but right then, the sweet silence felt good on them. It was as if they'd known each other for a hell of a lot longer than a few hours.

Yep. He was totally in trouble.

"What are you in the mood to eat?" he asked.

"I thought you had all the plans worked out," she teased, and he smiled. She was losing that ice shield, and he was loving it.

"You should know that, beyond ink and this night, my plans in life are more of a vague guideline."

Shea stopped suddenly, and he stopped with her.

"What is it?"

"I need plans, Shep. I like plans. I like schedules and calendars and color-coded things. They make me happy. When things are organized just so, the world is a better place. You should know that."

"You're a touch OCD, aren't you?"

"For me, when it comes to schedules it's more CDO." At his blank look, she smiled. "It's OCD, but the letters are in the right order. As they should be." Her lips twitched, and he threw his head back and laughed.

His calm, collected Shea was shitting with him.

Oh yes, tonight was gonna go fucking perfect—not matter what happened from here on out.

"Okay, so next time, I'll let you know where I want to take you, and then you can plan your outfit and what exactly we do for the night. How about that?"

She leaned into him, her eyes dancing, the joy there free and uninhibited. "That sounds perfect."

He smiled and took her lips again, unable to help himself. She sank against him, her body going lax. He slid his hand down the back of her dress to her ass and squeezed. Oh yeah, a perfect handful. His tongue tangled with hers and she opened wider, moaning.

"What's happening, Shep?" she asked once they pulled away from each other.

"I have no clue, Shea, but I can't wait to find out."

CHAPTER FOUR

"Shea, baby, arch your hips up. Let me see that pussy of yours."

Shea did as she was told, her moans breaking through her lips, her body writhing.

"Fuck, Shea, I can't wait to fill that pretty pussy of yours and feel you on my cock as you come around me."

Shea gasped at his words, wanting to come but unable to.

The phone rang, and she opened her eyes.

Well, crap.

She was tangled in her sheets, her nightie up around her waist and her panties at her ankles.

Shep was nowhere to be seen.

Well, he wouldn't be here, would he?

No. After an amazing night of listening to jazz music, eating sandwiches while standing in the street, and going from bar to bar, drinking, kissing, and laughing, he'd taken her home and kissed her goodnight on her doorstep.

They knew he wanted to come in.

They knew she would let him.

And they knew it wasn't the right time.

Her dreams, however, had other ideas.

Her body ached from lack of release, and it took all that she had not to pick up her phone and dial Shep so he could come help her.

Oh crap. That totally didn't sound like the Shea she knew. On the other hand, it was totally the Shea she wanted to be.

Her phone rang again, and she cursed, turning over on her stomach to reach for it on her nightstand, pulling up her panties at the same time.

It was six thirty, and she'd been out until almost two.

There was no way the person on the line would be the one she wanted it to be, so it was either her mother or Richard.

Not answering either one would just annoy them and they would eventually annoy her.

She looked at the display, cursed just like Shep would have, and answered, her voice icy.

"Mother."

"Sleeping after six am? I don't understand why you act this way. It's as if you've forgotten all of your training. I spent years on you and now look at you. Worthless. You could have married well at a young age and to Richard. He comes from a good family. Now look what you've done. You're nothing but an accountant who sleeps in like a whore."

Shea closed her eyes. Why had she answered her phone? She could have put it on silent and slept in just a bit more with the Shep of her dreams.

"Mother."

"Yes. I'm your mother, for all the good it has done. I gave you good breeding, a roof over your head, and a future so bright and filled with promise that I should have won awards for it. And yet what do you do? You leave all of that to work with numbers and become some tramp who lives alone and sleeps in with god knows who."

Her mother's fantasies of her life were much more enjoyable than the reality.

Just saying.

"Mother. Good morning to you too." Honestly, there really wasn't anything else to say when her mother started one of her tirades.

"It would have been a good morning if you'd been the daughter I wanted you to be. Not the daughter you are."

Ouch.

No, she hadn't said anything different than what she'd been saying for years, but still...

Ouch.

"Is there a reason you called this morning?" It was Sunday, after all. Since it was normally a day of rest, Mrs. Reginald Little the Third should at least be preparing to cut down other women at tea while not actually looking as though she was doing the cutting, *not* bothering her only daughter.

Her mother gave a long, drawn-out sigh. Seriously, the woman had that down to an art form.

"You're expected at brunch this morning. Richard will be there, and you can apologize. Hopefully, he will be gracious enough to take you back. I've worked all I can at this point to make up for your failures. Don't disappoint me by being yourself."

Shea ran a hand through her hair, the pang at her mother's familiar words like a sharp lance across her chest

"I can't go today, Mother." *Or any day.* "I have plans." Her plans with Shep weren't until later in the day, but her mother didn't need to know that.

"Plans? You?" Her mother laughed, and Shea winced. "Honey, you don't need to lie to me. I know you have no plans. Who would want to be with you? Now get dressed and wear something I've picked out for you. It won't do you any good to look like a whore in front of Richard. Look demure but make sure your breasts are high. He likes breasts. Once he gets a good look at what you have—which isn't that much, honestly—you can use those whore wiles of yours to get him to put that ring on your finger."

There wasn't enough freaking coffee in the world to deal with this.

Seriously?

She had to be both a whore and demure to keep a man she didn't want?

Jesus, did her mother even listen to herself?

"On that note, Mother, I'm hanging up now."

"Don't you be an ungrateful brat. I've done *everything* for you, and this is how you repay me? I will see you at brunch, or there will be hell to pay."

Shea hung up as her mother continued her tirade—something she wouldn't have done even two days ago.

It seemed laughing at night on the street with a man who held her close had helped her more than she thought. Just the idea of having a plan for that night—even if it was her job to make the plan more concrete—was worth any amount of yelling her mother would do later.

Although she would have liked to sleep in, she couldn't now. Not with the oily feeling sweeping over her at that early morning phone call.

She'd just have to get up and begin her day.

Shea showered, ate breakfast, and then planned their date for that night at the Preservation Hall. When Shep told her where they were going, she'd blinked. It wasn't a real date-like place, but he wanted to take her anyway. He said they'd do dinner and...other things afterward.

She blushed when she thought about what those other things could be.

Shea might not be the whore her mother thought she was, but she was ready to see what happened with Shep. She couldn't help herself.

By the time late afternoon rolled around, she was dressed

and ready to go. Shep would be there any minute to pick her up. Unlike the previous night when they'd arrived separately, she was fine with him knowing where she lived. Considering he'd dropped her off at her doorstep the night before, it was a little late to be worried about that.

Also, unlike the previous night, she wasn't dressed like an assistant or someone going to a high-end cocktail party.

Nope.

She'd had to search in the back of her closet for her outfit and luckily had enough on her "never-going-to-happen" rack, that she could be comfortable. She wore skinny jeans, a cute blouse, and those black fuck-me pumps she'd told Shep about.

She usually wore those with a dress, but she wanted to be a little daring today.

Hopefully he'd like it.

Damn it! She had to stop doubting herself. It had taken only one phone call from her overbearing shrew of a mother for her to revert back to the adolescent she'd been.

She was not that person anymore.

She just had to remember that.

A knock on the door pulled her out of her thoughts, and her hand went to her neck, her pulse fluttering.

He was here.

Okay, Shea, you can do this.

She smoothed out her top, her heart speeding the entire time. When she opened the door, she sucked in a breath—her usual reaction to seeing him.

He wore another dark button-up shirt that clung to him in all the right places.

He was beautiful.

Freaking beautiful.

"I knew you'd look fucking amazing in jeans, and I was not wrong. Not by a long shot."

Shep's words slid over her, and she sighed.

Yes. Sighed like a schoolgirl, and she didn't care.

She ran her hands down her jeans, still not sure she was wearing the right thing—even with Shep's obvious approval.

Jesus, she needed to get control over her insecurities. She wasn't sitting in her mother's living room being yelled at for spilling punch on her dress or for not wearing the latest fashions. Tonight she could not have cared less.

A hand palmed her cheek and forced her to gaze at Shep's face. He frowned, his brows lowering.

"What's wrong, baby? Too crass for you?"

She blinked, confused. "Oh, no. I don't mind what you said."

She blushed. "I *liked* what you said."

He let out a breath then brushed her cheekbone with his thumb. She sucked in her lips, loving the feel of his touch a little too much.

"Then tell me what's going on in that head of yours. You were a million miles away, and it didn't look like you were in a good place. What's wrong, baby?"

"Nothing," she lied. She always lied when it came to her mother and her *issues*. She didn't want to put a damper on their date any more than she already had. He didn't need to know that her mom was a psychopath who beat her daughter down with words every chance she got.

Her mother didn't know Shea had a storm brewing beneath the calm exterior.

She wanted to be different, but was too afraid to be that way.

She'd shut her true self away for so long she didn't know how to get back out.

Shep tilted her face up then brushed her lip with his thumb. "You don't have to lie to me, Shea. We're supposed to be getting to know each other, remember?"

"For my tattoo. You don't need to know everything, Shep."

"Baby, you know it's more than the tattoo. It's been more than the tattoo since you ran into me on the street and I couldn't breathe when I stared into those gorgeous eyes of yours. Yes, I will give you the best tattoo in the world. You're already so beautiful that anything I put on your skin will only enhance the art. But that's not all. I also want to find out what makes you tick, to know you. Last night we didn't talk about tattoos or designs. We talked about who we are. What we want. I don't want to go back. I'm here now because I want to know you, and I *know* you want to know more about me. Don't pull away now, Shea. Talk to me."

This man.

Damn it.

He took all she had and gave so much more back.

How the hell did he do that?

Leaning on him would take too much from her, but, hell, she wanted to do it.

"I'm sorry."

He shook his head in a quick jerk. "No. You don't get to be sorry, Shea. You're not doing anything wrong. Don't you understand? I want to know you. Every part of you. I can't do that if you close up and hide behind your apologies."

"Shep…"

"Talk to me, precious. What was on your mind that took you so far away? Why are you hiding from me? I know we haven't known each other long, but can't you feel it? That connection that means more than just a passing glance?"

She closed her eyes. "Yes. I feel it."

"Look at me, Shea."

She did, his piercing blue eyes taking her in.

"Tell me what happened."

"My mother is a bitch."

He blinked, and she held back a snort.

"That was a little blunt," she said.

"Uh, yeah. I'm not disagreeing with you on the bitch part, though, if she's making you feel like you looked just then." He moved, tugging her to her couch. "Tell me about it."

She loved the way he looked in her house, his tattoos and devil-may-care looks against her prim and proper decorating. He could totally dirty it up but in the best way possible.

She sank into the cushions like she had before, but this time, Shep pulled her even closer. The heat from his body scorched her, and she took it all in.

Oh yes, she wanted this.

Wanted him.

She just had to figure out a way to say it.

"Well, like I said, my mother is a bitch. No matter what I did as a kid, and even as an adult, it has never been good enough for her. I was born to be a debutante, to be the personification of the Little name, to use our money and influence to gain even more money and influence. From a young age, I've known that I was to be a pawn in my family's political and power games. I was born to marry well—to whomever they chose—and to be the best wife I could be. I wasn't taught to cook, but how to order servants around. I wasn't taught to clean, but to live in a pristine house taken care of by other people."

She took a deep breath, the resentment that she'd always tried to hide filling her.

Shep brushed a lock of hair from her face, and she leaned into his touch, needing him more than she dared admit.

"I'm not that person, Shep. At least, I've tried not to be that person. This house? I paid for it on my own. It's small, too small for my mother, who tells me that repeatedly. It's only two bedrooms, but fits me wonderfully. The things you see in it? They're all my mother. I couldn't stop her from decorating it so it would at least look 'decent' for her. I tried, but she found a way in and decorated when I was away for work."

"Jesus. She wouldn't even let you have a little bit of yourself in it?"

"Who am I, Shep? You're trying to figure it out for ink...and because you want to," she added as he narrowed his eyes. "I don't even know who I am. I'm trying to figure it out though. I *want* to figure it out."

Her chest constricted then lessened as she said the words she'd been afraid to.

"I want to grow beyond the person my mother has deemed me to be and failed at being for her. I...I just don't know how to do that. And, no, I didn't tell you all she's said to me, even what she said this morning, but I'm ready to move on. I have to."

Shep moved on the couch so he faced her. "Damn, baby. I want to know what your mother said to you to make you hide like that, but I'll wait. Now, as for finding yourself? God, woman, you're already shining through. I can't wait for you to find out who you are because I'm seeing her right now and liking it."

"Really?" She smiled, liking that he was so passionate about his words.

"Really, baby."

She moved then, cupping his face with her hands. "I don't want to go out tonight," she blurted out.

A look of hurt crossed his face before he smoldered, his eyes darkening, a slow smile crawling over his face. "Oh really?"

"Really."

He traced a finger along her cheek, and she shuddered. "What do you want to do tonight, baby?"

She traced her hand along his beard, loving the way his scruff brushed her skin. It made her wonder what it would feel like on other parts of her body.

She felt herself blush, and Shep chuckled, a rough sound that shot straight to her pussy.

"I take it by that blush you have an idea of what you want to do tonight. Let me guess. Does it involve me licking every inch of your body, sucking on those nipples and that sweet pussy of yours, then filling you with my cock?"

She swallowed hard. "That sounds like a plan," she croaked out.

"Do you know what you want first?"

Would asking for all of it be too much? Too brazen?

"Anything. Just tell me what to do."

By the way he groaned, she knew she'd said the right thing.

"Fuck yeah. Just do what I tell you and you'll come hard, baby. You'll love every minute of it."

She squirmed in her seat. "I already do."

"Hell yeah, you do."

Shep took her lips, his tongue sliding along the crease then tangling with her own. She moaned into his mouth, wanting, no, *needing,* more. He nibbled and licked along her lips then kissed down her jaw to bury his face in her neck. She arched toward him, wanting him to bite, suck...do *something*.

His hands found her breasts through her top, and she pressed her body closer.

"You like it?"

She just moaned, unable to speak.

"I'm going to fuck these pretty breasts of yours, Shea. Maybe not tonight, but soon. They're more than a handful, perfect for my cock. I can't wait to see my dick sliding between them as you hold them together. Maybe

I'll even fuck your mouth at the same time so your plump lips will lick and suck the crown of my dick as I fuck your breasts."

Jesus, the man was good at dirty talk.

She was about to come just by listening to him.

He stood up, bringing her with him. "Let's get these clothes off so I can see you. All of you."

She swallowed hard. She wasn't ashamed of her body, though she knew she wasn't the skinniest of girls. Her breasts were still perky, but not as high as they'd been when she was younger. Once she'd reached thirty, her body had curved and started to settle. She could only fight gravity for so long without losing a few battles.

Shep put a finger under her chin and forced her gaze to his. "Eyes on me, Shea. Stop with the doubt. You're fucking sexy, and I want to see you naked. Got it? You're beautiful, so stop thinking that you're not."

She smiled then reached for the bottom of her blouse. Shep's hands covered hers.

"No, let me."

He slowly tugged her shirt over her head then threw it behind him. "Jesus, Shea. How many layers are you wearing?"

She smiled at the annoyance in his tone. Apparently he wanted her naked quickly. Well, so did she.

"Just this cami and a bra. Then my jeans and panties. Oh, and my boots and socks."

Shep just shook his head then lowered his head to capture her lips. "I don't mind, baby. It just makes the anticipation that much sweeter."

Shea huffed out a breath. "Any more anticipation and I'll combust."

"Oh, honey, just you wait."

She gulped. "That's what I'm afraid of."

He divested her of her cami then knelt before her. He shucked off her boots quicker than she would have thought possible, tugged off her socks, and then slid her jeans down her legs, leaving her in her matching bra and panties.

He stayed kneeling in front of her, his gaze openly hungry. "Gotta say, Shea, love the fucking pink bows on black lace."

She blushed and lowered her head. She loved wearing sexy things under her clothes, and now that she'd seen that hungry look on Shep's face, she'd be sure to *always* wear something sexy for him.

At least underneath her clothes.

His calloused fingers slid up her body as he stood, bringing her closer. "God, Shea, you're beautiful."

He took her lips before she could answer, leaving her breathless.

His fingers made quick work of her bra, and he tossed it over his shoulder. Her breasts fell, heavy, her nipples already hard little peaks.

He brushed his thumb over one peak, plucked it, then did the same to the other. She arched, wanting more.

"Look at these nipples of yours, baby. Like berries, suckable, ready for my tongue." He bent down, captured one in his mouth, and sucked.

Her pussy clenched, and she moaned.

Hell, he felt so good.

His tongue flicked her nipple, and then he bit down gently. The shocking sting went straight to her core, and she rubbed her legs together, needing release.

He pulled back and gripped her hips. "No you don't. You don't get to make yourself come. That's my job. My treat."

"Shep."

He had to be kidding.

She needed to come.

Now.

"Nope. Go sit on the couch and spread your legs, baby."

She sucked in a breath at the order, but did as she was told. The quicker she did it, the faster Shep would let her come. It didn't make sense to dawdle.

She sank into the cushions, blushed, and spread her legs so he could see how drenched her panties were. There would be no hiding from him now.

"Jesus. You're so fucking wet I can see it with your panties on. You want this as much as I do."

"I want it more," she said, leaving herself vulnerable.

"Oh, honey, I don't think it's a competition. We'll tie in this." He sank to his knees, fully clothed, and pressed his face to her pussy, inhaling.

"Shep!" She tried to close her legs and move away, but he pressed her thighs with his large hands, keeping her open.

"Nah-uh, baby. You smell so fucking sweet. I can't wait to taste you."

He twisted his fingers in the sides of her panties and tugged them down her legs. He tossed those over his shoulder too.

The man was really working on making a mess of her house in short order.

All thoughts of a clean house and her clothes fled her mind when Shep lowered his head and took one long swipe along her clit.

Her butt rose off the couch, pressing her heat closer to his face. He pushed her back down then went to work, licking, sucking, and nibbling. He licked around her clit then moved the hood back to suck hard.

Her body shook, her legs going numb as she came with that one lick.

Her arms tingled, and her pussy clenched, wanting more.

Jesus, the man was good.

"Fuck, Shea, you came so hard, so quick. I knew you'd be responsive, but hell. I'm going to make you do it again. And again. Got me?"

"Whatever you say," she rasped out, too much in her pleasure zone to care.

He went back to what he was doing before and licked along the seam of her lower lips before moving his hand so his fingers found her wet, aching center.

He pumped his finger within her pussy then added two more as he sucked her clit. Her body, already high from her previous orgasm, shook then tightened as she rose again. He fucked her with his fingers and moaned against her. His beard scraped against the soft skin of her inner thighs, and she came, the sensation too much for her to hold back.

She'd never come like that during sex.

Let alone more than once.

And she hadn't even seen him naked yet.

Go, Shep!

No. Go, *Shea*!

He moved back and kissed up her body until he found her mouth. Her limbs heavy, she used all her strength to tangle her fingers in his hair. She could taste herself on his lips, and it made her even hotter.

"That was amazing," she whispered.

"You haven't seen anything yet." Shep pulled back and stripped.

Her eyes greedily took his body in. He was broad, built, tan, muscular...perfect. His tats covered his arms, thighs, and chest. They were fucking hot. He also had a little tat on his hipbone she knew she'd have to lick later.

Her gaze caught the metal adorning him, and she blinked. "You're pierced."

Shep chuckled and ran a hand over the barbells in his nipples. "Yeah, and I can't wait to have your tongue on them."

Her gaze lowered, and she swallowed hard.

"It's a dydoe piercing," Shep explained. He had two barbells on the top of his cock near the tip. They weren't that large in respect to his cock, but damn, it had to have to hurt.

"Didn't they hurt?"

"Hell yeah, but it's worth it. You'll see. The piercings will hit that one spot in that sweet pussy of yours, and you'll never want to leave my cock."

She bit her lip and squirmed on the couch. "What about if I...." She blushed. Jesus. She'd just had the man's mouth on her pussy, yet she couldn't say the words.

"Later, when I fuck that mouth of yours and have that little tongue run up and down my cock, you'll see. You don't have a tongue ring, so it won't be a problem if you give me head while I have the piercings in."

She blinked up at him. "So if I were to get a tongue ring?" Not that she'd ever thought about it, but she knew from others that tongue rings meant amazing blow jobs—there, she at least thought the word—for men. And if what she was thinking was right, Shep's piercings were for her, not for him. It would only be right to return the favor.

She squirmed again.

"Fuck, baby. If you do that, then I'll take them out when you want to go down on me. Right now though? Now I want to fuck you hard because I'm about to blow. You get me?"

Oh, she totally got him.

He pulled her up to her feet, steadied her, and then sat down on the couch. She watched as he rolled a condom down his length.

"Where did you get that?"

"It was in my jeans pocket, baby. If you hadn't been paying so much attention to my cock—not that I mind—you would have seen. Now hop on. Ride me."

She smiled and did as she was told, straddling his thighs.

His cock brushed her pussy, and she gasped.

"Holy shit, Shea. You're so fucking wet." Shep met her gaze, and she sucked in a breath, waiting.

She placed both hands behind his head on the couch, bracing herself. Shep's hands palmed her ass, squeezing, teasing.

Slowly, their gazes never wavering, she slid down his cock, the wide girth stretching her, but since she'd just come twice, she was slick and ready for him.

She rocked her hips slightly as she sank onto him, and he sucked in a breath. Yes, he liked that. Finally, she was fully seated, and she had to sit for a moment, trying to get used to the feel of him deep within her.

"This is heaven, Shea. Pure, fucking heaven."

She agreed, but she couldn't speak. Not right then. Finally, when she could breathe, she rocked again then slid up his cock.

"Jesus," he breathed.

She went slowly up then slammed back down, loving the way both of them gasped at the same time.

"Do that again."

"Of course," she whispered.

She repeated the action, over and over. Shep kept one hand on her ass, balancing her, while the other hand roamed, palming her breast then moving down to slide over her clit. She never let her gaze leave Shep's though. While she would have loved to throw her head back, close her eyes, and ride him like a cowgirl, right then, all she wanted to do was have this moment with him.

Have him know what he did to her.

From the look on his face, he knew.

She quickened the pace, feeling her inner walls tighten, her breasts grow heavy, and that tingle racing up her spine.

"Come now, Shea. I'm gonna go with you."

Needing no other motivation, she came hard, her pace never slowing. She felt Shep come inside the condom buried within her even as he shouted her name.

Their gazes locked and never broke.

"Let's do that again," Shea breathed.

Shep rocked his hips, and she moaned. "Give me two minutes, and I'll go fuck you on your bed. You've come three times, so I'll do all the work."

"Sounds like a plan," she said into his neck.

"Damn straight."

INK INSPIRED

And he totally did most of the work when he fucked her on her bed a few minutes later. She helped though.
Some.

CHAPTER FIVE

Shep groaned, images of the previous week's activities filling his mind. He leaned against the shower stall, needing to breathe. Jesus, he'd spent the past week working or by Shea's side.

Or inside Shea.

Yeah, he liked that part too.

He needed to stop thinking about the way she made those

little moans and how her body flushed all over as she wiggled on his cock. He needed to get to the café to meet Austin, and going there with a fucking hard-on wouldn't be the best thing.

But *fuck*.

The image of Shea on her knees, his cock tapping against her lips, and her fingers in her pussy as she fucked herself filled his mind.

He gripped his cock, using the soap he'd just used on his body to slide up and down the length. He squeezed hard then fucked his hand harder. He closed his eyes, imagined his hand was Shea's warm little mouth, that each squeeze was her hollowing her cheeks, sucking him hard, that each movement of his thumb on the crown was her tongue darting out, licking and tasting him.

Shea gave fucking great head, and she knew it now. Those losers she'd dated before didn't know the gem they'd had. Oh yeah, they knew she was hot because there was no denying that, but the fact that she laughed and gave great head made him want more.

Oh yeah, she was perfect for him.

He pumped his hips, fucking his fist while imagining Shea's pretty lips around his cock, her fingers finding that plump flesh between her legs.

He came hard, throwing his head back against the shower wall, his seed spilling to the floor as the water washed it down the drain.

Holy fuck.

Now he was rubbing one off in the shower like some damn high school kid even though he was regularly getting laid.

Shea would be the death of him, but what a way to go.

He finished washing up, his cock still semi-hard, but that seemed to be the norm when he was thinking about Shea, around Shea, or just breathing.

After he pulled on some clothes, he made his way to the café where Austin would be waiting. His cousin had shown up two days before, but instead of staying with him, he decided to stay with another of their friends.

Apparently Austin wanted to give Shep some time with Shea.

He'd take it.

Austin was sitting underneath one of the covered tables on the patio, sipping his coffee, a grin on his face that couldn't hide the weariness. Something was going on with his cousin, and Shep didn't know what to do about it or even if he *should* do something about it.

Hopefully, staying in New Orleans at least for a couple weeks to chill would help with whatever the heck was going on.

"It's about time you showed up," Austin said then took another sip of his coffee. Shep sat down next to his cousin, tired as all hell since he hadn't had enough sleep. "Your coffee by the way? Fucking amazing. I mean Denver is all about clean air and health. I love the brews, the microbrews, the views, everything. I wouldn't change it for anything. But down here? Coffee is pure decadence. Pure indulgence."

The waitress came over, and Shep held up two fingers. Shea was joining them soon, and the waitress knew what Shep liked. The little redhead smiled prettily, her eyes an open invitation, but he just smiled and shook his head.

She walked away, still smiling, but not as brightly.

"She tried that flutter and smile with me as well," Austin said as he lay back in his chair, the tattoo on his shoulders peeking around the collar of his shirt.

"And you didn't take her up on it? You're losing your touch."

Austin raised a brow. "You didn't either. And it's too early in the day for that shit. Plus, she's like what, twenty? Technically, she could be our kid."

Shep groaned. "Jesus. Why the fuck did you say that? Now I feel really old. And I didn't take her up on that because I'm with Shea. There's no way I'd skip out on her for anything, let alone that."

He shut his mouth as the waitress set down the two drinks, her eyes still inviting.

"Thanks," Shep said, his voice gruff. If she didn't take the hint, then he'd say it, but she should be able to read signals if she was going to flirt like this in public.

"I'm here if you need me. For *anything*."

She fluttered her eyelashes and sauntered off.

"Jesus. I am officially too old for this shit."

Austin gave a rusty chuckle. "Good to know you want to stay faithful to Shea. Not saying you've ever cheated—I don't do that shit either. But it's still good to know where this is heading."

"Why don't you just ask me what you're fishing for?" Seriously, the Montgomerys were always up in all the family's business. It didn't matter that Shep was far away. He was still family.

Austin took another sip. "Things serious between you and

Shea? You're not getting any younger, you know."

"We're the same age, so stop bringing up the old man crap. And as for me and Shea?" He sat back and thought about it. He'd had a couple of serious relationships before, but nothing that'd made him want to rush to the altar or picture the woman round with his child. Shea though? She was different. "Yeah, it's serious."

"Good to know, man. Good to know." Austin's gaze brightened as he looked over Shep's shoulder. "And here she is. Hey, Shea. Good to see you again."

They'd met when Austin had first come to New Orleans. He'd taken one look at her and announced he was staying at another friend's rather than Shep's.

Good man.

Shep turned and sucked in a breath.

Yeah, he was falling for that sexy blonde woman in the red dress.

Fast.

If he looked carefully enough, he might just find that he'd already fallen for her, but he knew both he and Shea weren't ready for that.

Yet.

The ruby red dress hugged her curves but went up to her neck in that same old-fashioned style she loved. She kept her flashes of skin just for him. The dress brushed the top of her knees, and this time she wore red flats rather than heels.

He'd told her they were going to need to walk today for their date, so she'd dressed just for him.

Yep, he totally was falling for her.

He stood and went to her, unable to wait any longer. He cupped her face and tilted it up to him. Her lips were barely open, and he took it as an invitation and captured her mouth.

Damn, he loved her taste.

He pulled back breathless and looked down at that sexy, flushed face. "Hey."

She grinned. "Hey."

"Hey to you both," Austin called from behind them. "Now sit down and stop making out on the street. Your coffee is getting cold, and I want to order beignets. I'll eat them all you know."

Shep turned, wrapped an arm around Shea's shoulders, and walked them toward Austin. "You eat all those and you'll lose your girlish figure."

Austin ran a hand over his flat stomach and grinned. "It'd totally be worth it."

Shea laughed, the sound filling his soul. God, the woman needed to laugh more, and he knew she was starting to do so. The ice was breaking, and the wild fire was burning.

His Shea was more than what her mother wanted her to be—much, much more.

"You got me coffee?" she asked.

He kissed her temple then relaxed back into his chair. "Yeah. It's the chicory that you love."

She grinned and took a sip, the little moan escaping from her mouth going right to his cock.

Out of the corner of his eye, he saw Austin grin, but he ignored the bastard. That little moan was just for Shep.

"So, where are we going this morning?" she asked after they ate their beignets.

"Well, I need to go into work for a bit like I said, and you said you were going to come with," Shep answered.

She smiled brightly but her eyes held a trace of nervousness. "I want to see how you work. You know, get ready for my own tattoo."

"It's good that you get used to the feel before you do something like that," Austin added. "Plus Shep is fucking phenomenal at his ink, so you're in good hands. If I didn't think so, I'd take care of you myself."

Shep frowned at his cousin. He had a feeling Austin was talking about more than ink when it came to Shea, but he didn't want to harp on it in front of her. That would be something he beat his cousin for later.

"I trust him completely," Shea said, and Shep sucked in a breath.

Fuck yes.
Finally.

"So, where are you taking me after you work?"

Shep grinned. "The St. Louis Cemetery."

Austin barked out a laugh while Shea's eyes widened.

"A cemetery? That's your idea of a date?"

Shep shrugged then stole a kiss. "You'll love it. I promise."

"I don't really like being scared, Shep."

He tugged her close. "Baby, it's not an amusement park where they try to scare you on certain rides. Here there's real history. We'll go for a bit. Take a look around. See something we wouldn't normally see. Then go home."

"Where Shep will be sure to keep you warm if you get too cold," Austin butted in dryly.

"Shut it, Austin," Shep bit out.

Shea grinned up at him. "Oh really? And just how will you keep me warm?"

He leaned down and bit her bottom lip. "Minx. Don't make me tell you in detail in front of Austin. We have to head to Midnight Ink, and I'm not gonna want to ink with a hard-on."

Shea snorted. "That would be awkward."

"Uh, yeah, considering I'm inking a sixty-year old woman today with her grandkids' names." Actually he was working their names into an intricate piece with lilies of the valley and lavender. He was revved up for it—something he hadn't been in a while.

Shea's eyes widened then she threw her head back and laughed. "Oh poor baby."

"Shut it, woman." He kissed her hard then stood. "I'll make you pay for laughing."

Her eyes darkened, and she licked her lips. "I'm sure you will."

Fuck. It was going to be a long day.

****

Shep closed the door behind them then pushed Shea against it. He wrapped her hair around his fist, pulled her head to the side, and buried his face in her neck.

She wiggled against him and laughed. "So, you said something about warming me up?" she said, panting.

He pulled back and rocked his erection against her. "Oh yeah. Were you scared when we walked amongst the dead tonight?"

She tried to move closer, but he pressed her to the door. "Let me touch you."

"Answer me, Shea."

"Of course, but you were there, so it wasn't that bad. Just hold me now, and I'll be okay."

He grunted, pressing his hips flat against hers. "I'll hold you, Shea. Don't forget that. I'm not letting go."

"Deal."

He smiled then lowered himself to the floor.

"What are you doing?"

"I'm going to eat you out with your leg wrapped around my shoulder. Then I'm going to fuck you against the door. Okay?"

"Oh. Okay," she rasped out, and Shep chuckled.

He knew Shea loved his head between her legs, his mouth on her pussy. She'd come hard when he'd done it the last time, so he was gonna do it every chance he had.

Even if that meant his cock might explode.

He helped her take off her shoes and tossed them behind him. If they had been heels, he would have made her wear them when he fucked her since that was hot as hell. That would just have to wait for another time.

He stripped her panties off and smiled. He loved the little triangle of pale blonde hair above her pussy. He just loved her pussy, actually.

All of it.

He spread her legs, wrapped one around his shoulder so she could have the other to support herself, then got to business. He licked around her clit, ran his hands up her thighs, and spread her lower lips so he could see that pink, glistening pussy.

Oh, yes.

He fucked her with his tongue then his fingers then his tongue again, her sweet taste coating his tongue. He heard her panting above him, so he kept his pace the same, not letting her come until he was finished.

Not that he'd ever get tired of eating her out.

He sucked on her clit while his fingers found that little bundle of nerves and pressed down. She came apart, her pussy tightening around his fingers like a vise.

He pulled away while she was still coming, pulled his cock out of his jeans, slid on a condom, then pistoned into her heat before she could gasp.

"Fuck, Shea, you're so tight."

"Oh, God. I love it. Please fuck me."

"That's my dirty girl."

He pumped his hips as she wrapped her legs around him. He

gripped her ass, keeping her against the door. He buried his face in her neck as she tugged on his hair, hard.

Her hips met his stroke for stroke, so hard that the sounds of their fucking echoed in the room. He didn't care.

He wanted her.

Now.

She let out a little gasp then tightened around him, coming. He slammed into her once more and came right behind her, his seed filling the condom.

He couldn't wait until he could go bare with her.

They stood like that for a few minutes, his cock still hard as if he hadn't just come. He wasn't a young man anymore, but, fuck, he knew he could go again if Shea wanted to.

Finally he pulled out and let her feet hit the floor. He left her for a second, ran to the kitchen to get rid of the condom, and came back into the room.

Her gaze met his then lowered to his cock.

"Go sit on the couch," she ordered, and he raised a brow.

"Shea..."

"Go sit on the couch," she repeated.

"You saying you want to suck me?" He'd totally be game for that.

"I totally give great head. Just saying." He laughed, loving the way she was starting to speak her mind and get dirty about it, a far cry from the Shea he'd first met.

He took off the rest of his clothes then stripped Shea's dress off. She gave a little yip, and he laughed before taking off her bra.

"I thought I was going to do you," she said, trying to sound firm.

"If you're going to suck me, I want to make sure those tits are free so I can play with them at the same time. Sound good?"

He watched her nipples tighten. "Sit. Couch. Now."

He strolled to the couch, his cock bobbing. Yep, heaven. Pure heaven.

As soon as he sat, Shea was there, kneeling between his thighs, a hungry expression on her face. He didn't have a chance to speak before she'd gripped his length and started stroking. He was still wet from coming so she could slide easily along his cock.

She smiled at him, her eyes inviting, then licked the slit at the stop of his cock. He sucked in a breath then watched—and *felt*—as she licked around the bar bells at the tip of his dick. She sucked along the length of him, rubbing him down where her mouth wasn't. Her mouth trailed to his balls and his ass left the couch, the pleasure increasing as she sucked one ball into her mouth, rolled it around, and then did the same to the other one.

"Fuck, you were right. You're totally amazing at giving head."

She pulled away and licked her lips. "And I haven't even sucked you down yet."

He swallowed hard, put his hand at the base of his cock to hold himself still, and lifted his chin. "I'm here, baby."

She grinned then took the crown of his cock into her mouth. She sucked down, and he about lost it. Jesus, she felt good.

She bobbed her head, each time taking more of him. What she couldn't swallow, her hands held and squeezed.

Unable to hold himself back, he wrapped her hair around his fist and pulled. She let him go with a pop and frowned.

"I was busy."

"I'm going to fuck your mouth, Shea. You okay with that?" He didn't want to hurt her.

Her eyes widened, and she nodded. He lowered her head to his dick, and she swallowed the tip then let her jaw relax. He tightened the grip on her hair, keeping her in place, then pumped his hips, slowly at first. The sight of his dick sliding in and out of her mouth had to be one of the hottest things he'd ever seen.

She kept her mouth wide so she didn't hurt herself on his piercings. If he wanted to go harder in the future, he'd have to take them out.

He fucked her mouth slowly, keeping a tight hold on her hair.

"Touch yourself, Shea. Make yourself come."

She nodded, his dick still in her mouth, and then slid her hand down her belly.

He pulled her head back and shifted so he could still pump into her and see her fingers go in and out of her pussy. Her fingers came back wet, and he almost came.

He tugged on her hair then fucked her mouth just a bit harder.

"Touch your clit, Shea. Pinch it." She moaned as she did. "Roll and pinch your nipples as you fuck your fingers, baby. I'm going to blow my load soon, and you have to come first. You got me?"

She nodded, eagerness in her eyes.

He watched as she fingered herself and played with her nipples, the sight intoxicating. Her breath came in pants around his cock until finally she moaned, her eyes rolling to the back of her head as she peaked.

"Relax and swallow, Shea."

Her gaze met his, and she nodded. He pumped into her mouth twice more then stayed there, his seed spilling on her tongue, down her throat.

Finally, he released her hair and pulled her into his lap. She curled into him, and he ran his hands over her body.

"You okay, baby?"

"Never better. You?" she whispered, her face in his neck.

"Heaven, Shea. Fucking heaven."

CHAPTER SIX

Shea swore the papers on her desk had multiplied over the weekend. She glanced at the stacks that hadn't been there on Friday and swore. Her co-workers were crazy if they thought she'd organize their mess.

Oh, *hell* no.

She might have rolled over and done it before, but not now.

Not since Shep.

Okay, so, according to Shep, it was all her and he'd had nothing to do with the fact that she was growing a backbone, but she'd take it.

He'd made her smile, lose herself and find herself, all in two weeks.

Two weeks.

She couldn't believe she'd known him for only two weeks. It didn't make any sense that she should feel what she felt about him—even if she wouldn't say the words—in such a small amount of time.

He made her laugh. He took her on the craziest dates. Who in their right mind would want to go to a cemetery in the middle of the night just to learn a bit more about their city and cuddle closer?

The image of just how close they got against the door, on the floor, in the bed, later in the shower, and then even later on the breakfast table, filled her mind.

She blushed so hard, she could feel the heat in her cheeks.

Oh yeah.

She liked the way he warmed her up in *every* way.

"There you are. Look at this mess. You chose to leave a perfectly good man for what? This squalor? I can tell from those piles on your desk you're behind. You're not even good at the job you left the family for, are you? God, what good are you?"

Shea froze at her mother's callous words.

What the hell was that woman doing here? She'd never once stepped foot inside Shea's office. Her place of work was too low class for a woman such as her mother—something Shea had secretly loved since that usually gave her a break from the bitch queen of all bitches.

"Mother?" she gasped, the flush from thoughts of Shep cooling faster than a plunge in the Arctic.

"Of course it's me. Who did you think it was? Is some other woman coming in here, knowing what I know? Of course you're probably disappointing other people just as you disappoint me, but just remember, you can *never* disappoint others like you disappoint me."

Shea had had enough.

"What is your problem, Mother? What have I ever done to deserve your scorn? You've beat on me since I was a little girl. Oh, you've never raised a hand to me. That would be too low-born. Yet you've never found me good enough. I've always been lacking. Tell me, Mother, what have I done?"

Her mother froze, her mouth gaping like a fish's before it thinned. "What have you done? Nothing!" She threw up her hands. "Nothing. You've always been a worthless leech. I've done all I could to ensure your place in our society. I've planned and perfected the perfect marriage, and yet look what you've done. You've thrown it all away. And for what? A tattooed thug who wouldn't be fit to lick my pumps."

Her mother knew about Shep?

"How the hell do you know about my boyfriend? And, for the record, don't talk about Shep like that. You know nothing about him."

"I know everything about him, darling. Don't you understand? I know all. It just takes a little money and a little shove and I know everything. I know about your trolling around town like a common trollop. He can't even take you on real dates. No. He takes you to places like cemeteries. God. He's an axe murderer waiting to happen, and you're cavorting with him? No. Not anymore, darling. Not anymore."

"You've had me followed?" Shea knew better than to assume her mother had followed her. There would be no way in hell her mother would lower herself to actually do the work on her own. Shea was surprised the woman had even taken the time to venture this far.

Something must be up the woman's sleeve.

Dread crawled up her spine, and she raised her chin, preparing herself.

"Of course I have. I've never stopped, Shea. You think you've left the family, but you haven't. We've let you take this break so you can *find* yourself, but now it's time to come back. Richard was understandably upset you couldn't make it to brunch, but he's still prepared to take you back. Of course we're compensating him for his trouble. It's only proper."

Shea blinked. "You've *paid* him to marry me? This isn't Regency England! I don't need a freaking dowry."

"Watch your mouth and keep a civil tone. Richard will have to strike that out of you if it continues."

Had her mother really just said her want-to-be-husband had to hit her? Jesus, the woman was certifiable.

"Mother—"

Her mother raised her hand, cutting her off. "No. I don't want to hear your excuses. You will leave this job immediately. You've already shown me that you can't keep up with the work. Just look at that messy desk of yours. A true Little would have at least excelled at their chosen profession. You couldn't even do that."

"That's not my work. I'm great at what I do. Stop cutting me down."

Her mother narrowed her eyes. "I don't like this new attitude of yours. At least when you left the family before, you did it with your eyes downcast like the little bitch you are. Now? Now I blame that tattooed thug for putting thoughts into your head. You're nothing, Shea. That thug is even less than you are. In another world, you two would be perfect for each other. Now? In this world, you're nothing. You're needed for the family, and you won't be allowed to slack on your responsibilities any longer. I won't have it."

Rage poured through her. "You won't have it? Who do you think you are? You're not my mother. You're just a shrewish bitch who doesn't understand she can't control me. Leave me alone. Can't you understand that I'm happier without the family? You'll notice not once have you mentioned Daddy's name. Why is that? Is it because he doesn't care one way or another? He's never cared, Mother. I don't care either. Just leave me alone."

Her mother flinched at the mention of her husband.

Direct hit.

Sadly, it didn't make Shea feel any better.

"Leave your father out of this. You've never been good enough for him either. You're the reason he ignores the things he does. You."

"Whatever you say, Mother. Now leave please. I'm tired and

have work to do. Then I'm going to see Shep because I'm thirty-two years old and far beyond the age of caring what my mother says. Especially when all she spews is vitriol and hate. I'm done."

Her mother's lips thinned even more. If the woman wasn't careful, she'd run out of lips to thin.

"You can try, Shea. Oh, you can certainly try. But if you don't meet Richard tonight for dinner and say yes to his offer, I'll ruin that thug, *Shep*, and everything he touches."

Shea froze. "What the hell do you mean by that?"

"Watch your language."

"Fuck my language!" she screamed. "Tell me what you mean. You can't hurt Shep. He means nothing to you. He's not part of *your* circles and thank God for that," she spat.

Her mother raised her chin. "Oh, yes, he's certainly not part of that. He'll never be part of that. But what he is, is a lowlife with no college education who does something prisoners do in a jail cell."

"Shep's art is brilliant. You know nothing about him. Stop putting him down."

"He's *nothing*. With just a few phone calls, I can close that harbor of harlots, Midnight Ink. I'll make it so he can't even draw with chalk on the street without the police on his back for some crime or another. I'll ruin him, Shea. Don't think I won't. And if you still refuse to stay away from him, I'll ruin that other shop in Denver, Montgomery Ink. I'll ruin them all."

The determined glint in her mother's eyes made Shea want to throw up.

As it was, bile filled her mouth, and she fought to control her shaking.

Jesus.

Who *was* this woman?

"You...you can't do that," Even to Shea's ears, she knew her voice sounded weak.

Of *course* her mother could do that. The woman lived for things like this. She had connections through money and the family everywhere.

Shep could actually lose everything because her mother was a selfish, vindictive shrew.

Jesus.

"You know I can, Shea. You know I'd crush him under my shoe without even batting an eyelash. I'd enjoy it too."

Shea swallowed hard. "Why? Why do you want to do this?"

"We need Richard's family," her mother snapped. "We might have money and power in this state, but Richard's has it throughout the entire country. Together we can go even further. You know Richard has political ambitions. With you by his side, our family will be in the hallowed halls for generations. We will be remembered. Eternal."

The woman had to be crazy. Certifiably insane.

"If you don't leave him, I'll take it all from him, Shea. You have until tonight."

With that, her mother turned on her expensive heels and left Shea standing alone in her office.

Broken.

Shea staggered back, her feet barely working as she bumped into her desk. A stack of papers fell to the floor, but she ignored them.

What was she going to do?

This couldn't be happening. Her mother couldn't just come

into her life and try to regain the control she'd had for so long.

Shea closed her eyes, the tears she hadn't noticed before falling harder.

She'd lose Shep.

To ensure his life remained as he knew it, to ensure his happiness, she'd lose him.

Her arms went numb, her chest tingling.

God.

She couldn't lose him. She'd just found him.

She'd finally stood up to her mother with her chin held high, and it was for naught. Her mother always had the upper hand, the ace up her sleeve, and now she had what would guarantee the end of the life Shea wanted to build with a man she loved.

No matter how much she thought she could fight it, her mother would fight harder to punish Shea for the faults and wrongdoings she'd never actually committed.

That was the type of woman her mother was.

Shea didn't know how to fight against it.

Oh, she might have learned to fight for herself and would fight to the ends of the earth for Shep, but to risking hurting Shep beyond measure fighting against her mother when she knew she couldn't win?

No.

She couldn't do that.

She'd have to in order to make sure he could live without her.

She'd marry Richard and break completely in the process.

She'd do anything for Shep.

Even leave him.

She cleaned up the stack of papers she'd dropped and put them on top of the other stack of papers that she'd leave to the other accountants.

Hell. She was really giving up.

This was the person her mother had made her, the person she'd fought so hard not to be.

She hated it.

"Shea? I brought coffee."

The sound of Shep's voice startled her, and she dropped the papers in her hand on the floor. She cursed again—inwardly reminding herself she'd have to stop that when she married Richard—and bent to pick them up.

"Oh, I'm sorry, baby, for scaring you. Here, let me help with that."

Out of the corner of her eye, she saw Shep put down two coffee cups and a bag of something and walk toward her.

She had to turn away.

It hurt too much to face him.

She would just have to slink away like the coward she was.

"I've got it. I'm actually kind of busy right now. You've caught me at a bad time." Her voice was ice, just like it had been before she'd walked into Midnight Ink the first time and clapped eyes on the man she'd fallen in love with.

"Hey, what's up? What's wrong?" He put his hand on her elbow, turning her toward him. She lowered her head, unable to meet his gaze. "Talk to me."

"You need to go, Shep." The words were torn from her, bile rising in her throat yet again.

He lifted her head with a finger on her chin. "Why, Shea? Why do I need to go?"

"You…you have to leave. This has been fun. It really has, but I need to go back to my life. I've changed my mind about the tattoo. I don't want it anymore. I don't want you anymore."

She held back the tears, the agony unbearable.

Pain flashed across Shep's face before his expression went carefully blank. "What?"

"I...I can't be with you anymore. We're different people. You're so...you. So vibrant. So...Midnight Ink. I am ice. I've always been ice, and I will always be ice. You need to go, Shep."

"What the fuck are you talking about, Shea?"

"You need to go, Shep. We can't see each other anymore. It's over."

He looked down at her, wearing that same expression he'd worn when she'd first asked for her tattoo at Midnight Ink.

"No."

CHAPTER SEVEN

"No," Shep repeated, keeping the anger—the anguish—at bay. "No. You don't get to do this."

"No? Why do you keep saying that? You can't just say no and get what you want." Her chin wobbled, and Shep clenched his jaw. Something was going on here, something more than fear of commitment or whatever he thought it might have been at first.

No, this was something much worse.

Shea was scared about something, and he'd be damned if he let her end it now because of it.

"I said no in the shop because you had no fucking clue what you wanted inked on your body, Shea. It's permanent. It's not a fucking dress or some shit like that."

Her head snapped back as though he'd slapped her, and he took a breath through his nose. Shit. He hadn't meant to lash out, but he was just so fucking angry that she was trying to leave him.

He'd never wanted a committed relationship before, yet now he wanted one.

With Shea.

She didn't get to leave.

Not when he knew she wanted the same thing.

Or least *had* wanted.

"I know a tattoo isn't a dress or pair of shoes, Shep. I'm not an idiot. Don't treat me like one."

"Then don't treat *me* like an idiot and lie to me. You're leaving because you're done with me? Fuck that. You're lying. Now tell me what the fuck is going on."

She swallowed hard, his gaze following the long lines of her throat. "I'm done, Shep. I don't want this." Her voice broke, but she didn't let the tears in her eyes fall. "Just go. Please."

He cupped her face, and she tried to move back. He tightened his grip, not enough to hurt, but to show her he wasn't letting her go.

Not without an explanation. Maybe not ever.

"You don't get to leave me, Shea. Not when I know you're leaving because you're scared. If you didn't want me anymore? I'd know. You wouldn't be on the verge of breaking down. Something scared you. What was it, baby?"

She closed her eyes. "Let me go, Shep. I...I can't do this. I can't let you get hurt."

Hurt?

"Tell me, Shea."

"I can't."

"Is it your family?" Her eyes opened, and she nodded. Okay. He was getting warm. "You aren't who your family is, Shea. You aren't the person your mother wants you to be." She flinched. "Baby, you're so much fucking more. You're a breath of fresh air and so fucking amazing that I want to find every single layer of your soul and wrap myself in it. I love you so fucking much, Shea. Can't you see that?"

Her breath quickened. "Don't say that, Shep. You can't mean that."

"Stop it. You don't get to tell me how I feel. I love you. I've never loved anyone other than my family, so don't tell me I'm wrong. I fucking *love* you."

"You're trying to tell me how I feel!"

"Because you're lying to yourself! You aren't the person your family thinks you are, or should be, Shea. You aren't who *you* think you are."

She sighed.

He was getting closer.

"I want you, Shea. I want everything. I want the woman I went with on those nights. I want the woman in the prim dress and fuck-me heels. I want everything."

"Shep."

"No, let me finish. I want you to get that tattoo. I want to mark your body with your soul then mark you with me. I want you to look down at yourself and know I love you."

The tears started falling.

"Then, baby, I want your brand on my body. I want you to look at me and know I love you."

"Shep."

"I want everything, Shea."

She pulled away and tried to go around him. He wrapped his arms around her middle, pulling her close so her back rested against his front. He pressed his nose to her nose and inhaled.

"Baby, tell me what's wrong."

"I can't." Her voice shook, and he broke for her.

"Baby, don't be scared. I'll be there to catch you, though you're strong enough to catch yourself, too. You just have to believe it."

Silence, then a whispered, "I-I'm not strong enough. I'm a c-coward." The tears fell in earnest now, and he turned her, crushing her to his body.

He ran a hand down her back while murmuring his love and promises.

"Baby, tell me what happened."

"My mother," she whispered, her voice dead.

His grip tightened. "Your mother?" What the fuck had the bitch done now?

"She..." Shea stopped, took a deep breath, and tilted her chin until she met his gaze. "She told me that if I kept seeing you, she'd destroy you."

"Destroy me? What the fuck? Does she think this is some B movie or something?"

Shea shook her head. "You don't understand. My family has connections. No, not mob connections or anything." She paused. "Actually, I don't know if that's true. But the thing is, they have money. Lots of money.

Mother uses that money to get what she wants."

"And what she wants this time is to break us up."

Shea bit her lip. "That and more."

"Why do I not like the sound of *more*?"

"She wants me to leave my job and meet Richard tonight."

"Richard. Your ex-fiancé, Richard?"

"That's the one. She says she's *paid* him to marry me. She *sold* me to gain more influence for the family."

He hugged her tighter. "Oh, baby. I love you, but I want to fucking kill your mom."

"You'll have to stand in line," she mumbled.

"Tell me about what she has on you for you to even consider this, Shea. I know you, baby. You left the family once, and yet you're going to go back to them?"

"Like I said. She's going to destroy you."

"How? Honey, she doesn't even *know* me. How can she destroy me?"

"She's going to have Midnight Ink shut down and make it so you can't work. Then she's going to hurt your family up in Denver, Austin and everyone. Shep, she's done things like this in the past. She had my third grade teacher fired and her license revoked because the woman stood up to her when Mother wanted me to do different work than the kids whose parents had less money than us."

"Jesus. What a fucking bitch. How the hell did she do that?"

"I don't know. Money solves a lot of problems for her. Shep, I don't want you to lose everything. I can't let that happen."

He kissed her. Hard.

When he pulled back, she looked up at him, her eyes dark.

"No. She doesn't get to do this. Fuck that. She might know people, but the people at Midnight Ink are even craftier than her. Fuck her. My family has influence too, baby. Not the same as her, but enough that she can't hurt us. I'll find a way to keep us safe, baby. You don't get to run from me in order to protect me. Got it?"

"Shep. I won't have her hurt you."

"Well, you don't get to decide that."

"You tell me to be independent and fight for myself. That's what I'm doing."

"No. You're fighting for me and doing a fucked-up job of it."

"Well, fuck you!"

Shep threw his head back and laughed.

"This isn't a time to laugh, Shep."

"Jesus, baby, you just told me to fuck myself. You, the one who doesn't like using curse words except when I'm buried deep inside you."

A slow blush crept over her skin. "Stop bringing that up."

"Baby, you look beautiful when you come. You look beautiful every day. You do not get to leave me because your mom is a bitch. I'll call a few guys at Midnight and get this taken care of. She doesn't have the power she thinks she does. We're not high up in the echelons of power. We're down and dirty. She can't play our game."

"You promise?" she asked, her voice so full of hope he broke for her.

"I promise. Don't leave me, Shea."

"I didn't want to. I want to stay with you. I want it all too." The last part was whispered.

"Jesus I love you so much." He kissed her hard then pulled back. "Do you have anything to say to me?" he teased.

Shea smiled, the tears in her eyes now of happiness rather than the pain he'd seen before. "I love you so much. So freaking much."

"Damn straight, woman. Now, you have the office to yourself for a bit?"

Shea frowned. "Yes. I'm alone today. Why?"

"Because I'm going to fuck you on your desk while you're wearing those pretty pink heels. Got a problem with that?"

Her eyes darkened, and she squirmed in his hold. "Shep..."

"Got a problem with that?" he repeated.

"No," she whispered.

INK INSPIRED

"Good. Take off your panties, Shea."

She gulped. "What about my skirt or shirt?"

"I want to keep you dressed. Doesn't that sound good? Me fucking you with us both dressed so when you go back to work later today, you'll be wearing my scent?"

She nodded and moved to slide down her panties.

What a sight.

Jesus.

He undid his jeans and took his cock out. Then he took the condom out of his back pocket—something he always had on him since meeting Shea—tore the package open, and slid it over his length.

"Bend over your desk, Shea."

She licked her lips and did what she was told. Her skirt was too long for him to see anything so he stood back and stroked his already hard cock.

"Hike up your skirt. Show me that pretty pussy."

Her arms reached around, and she slid her skirt up to her hips, keeping her cheek to the desk. Hell, his woman knew what he wanted.

The act left her ass and pussy bare for him.

"Spread your legs a bit, baby. I want to see all of you."

She did so, her legs shaky in her high heels, but she looked damn gorgeous.

Her ass was round, firm, yet with enough give that he always had a nice grip when he pumped into her. Her pussy was wet just from his voice, and he couldn't wait to sink his cock into it. Usually, he'd eat her out and go slow, but right now, he wanted her around his dick.

He stalked toward her and rested one palm on her ass. He moved and slapped it hard.

"Shep."

"Never leave me again. Don't even think about it. Not when it's for something as stupid as what happened."

She nodded, and he soothed the spot he'd slapped. They didn't play with spanking, other than a few here or there, but from the way she'd gasped when he did it, it would be something for them to look forward to in the future.

He let the tip of his cock rest against her folds, and she sighed. She tried to push back, taking more of him, but he held her firmly.

"Not yet, Shea. Let me control it."

"Anything, Shep."

God, he loved this woman.

He positioned himself then slammed into her with one thrust.

She arched back, a scream in her throat. Her pussy constricted around him as she came.

"Jesus, Shea. You came with just one touch. You're fucking hot, you know that?"

"You do it to me, Shep. Now, please, fuck me. Make me yours."

Well, if that's what she wanted.

He pulled back slowly then entered her just as fast as he had before. He gripped her hips and fucked her hard, pumping into her as fast as he could. Sweat beaded his forehead as he fought to keep from coming.

He didn't want this to end.

No, he wanted the image of Shea bent over her desk, his dick sliding in and out of her pussy, ingrained on his mind forever.

His balls tightened, and he cursed before pulling out of her.

"What?" she asked before he flipped her on her back and entered her in one stroke. "Oh," she gasped.

"I want to see your face when I come." He tangled the fingers of one hand with hers, the other on her ass to keep her steady. She wrapped her legs around his waist, heels and all.

He pumped into her as he kissed her, trailing his lips on every part of her he could reach. They were both still wearing clothes, and he knew as soon as he could, he'd strip them both so they could touch skin to skin.

His dick throbbed, ready to explode, and he took her mouth one more time.

"Love you, Shea."

"Love you, Shep."

He slammed once more into her, his come filling the condom

as he groaned her name into her neck.

"Best. Ever," Shea panted.

He grinned against her. "You haven't seen anything yet."

EPILOGUE

"It rubs the lotion on its skin..."

Shep froze, one hand on Shea's side, the other on her bare bottom, keeping her in place. He repressed a shudder and closed his eyes.

"Shea, baby, stop saying that every time I put lotion on your tattoo."

She twisted around so he could see her face. The action brought her breasts closer to him so he leaned down to lick one peak.

He couldn't help himself.

Shea moaned and wiggled in his hold. He squeezed her ass then spanked her hard. "Keep still."

"You just spanked me!"

"You keep making that creepy movie reference when I rub you down with lotion."

She snorted and shook her head. "Sorry. It just comes to mind whenever you're lubing up my tattoo."

"And stop calling it lube. We've had to be careful for months so I wouldn't hurt you when I fucked you, so don't get me hard now."

Shea pouted, and Shep laughed. Oh yeah, he loved this new playful Shea. Sure, she could still be the ice princess when she needed to be, but whenever it was just the two of them, she was pure silk.

Pure *his*.

Together, they'd broken ties with Shea's family for good. That damn mother had no idea who she'd been trying to mess with. The Montgomerys and the people of Midnight Ink did not bow to anyone. It had taken only a few calls and they had enough dirt on Mr. and Mrs. Little to bury them forever. It was amazing what money for drugs and the need for kink—kink that wasn't within the boundaries of the law—could do to a family that prided themselves on being proper.

Apparently being proper was only for the cameras.

He'd chosen to keep that close to the vest though. There was no way he'd hurt Shea in the process of taking out her parents.

He'd had the people at Midnight blackmail them. Yes, Shea knew everything to the last detail, even though she'd hated it, but nothing would blow back on her.

The Littles relented, and Shea had broken free.

She was free to be herself, to be with him, and to get her ink.

He ran a hand over the piece that had taken two very long sessions to complete. Shea had been a trooper, only wincing a couple of times before she fell into a rhythm with the buzz of the needle.

Oh yeah, he totally fucking loved this woman.

His finger traced the cherry blossom tree that ran up her entire right side and smiled. A branch curved under her breast and he knew that had hurt like a bitch, but she hadn't complained. Another branch ran up to her shoulder so it peeked out of dresses she wore. The tree's limbs tangled around the trunk and down across her hip, flowed across her lower back and ended right above her ass.

Seriously, it was his best piece of work ever.

Each bloom was a delicate form of pink, white, and shading.

The cherry blossom symbolized the end of winter, a difficult time, or a journey that had taken its toll. They'd chosen the cherry blossom tree because of her change and the way she wanted to live life.

Free.

She blossomed without her family's influence, so it was only fitting he'd done this for her.

What made that tattoo perfect for them were the carvings within the trunk of the tree. He hadn't gone for the normal fill and shading but had sketched markings that were special to them, leaving room in certain areas to add more when they occurred.

There was a Celtic marking for joy right on her ribcage. He remembered her laugh, her smile, her pure joy on their first date while listening to the bands play.

Another marking was Celtic for fearless. She'd run through the cemetery with him, jumped head first into his world, and brightened it for him. She'd gotten one of the largest tats he'd ever done on her first try because that's who she was.

The final marking was for freedom. That was the easiest thing to put on her body. She was finally free, though her freedom did come with him attached.

Not that she minded.

He rested his hand on her side and looked down at her. "I love you, Shea."

"I love you too, Shep. Though now that I'm fully healed, I'd love you more if you'd finally get down to business like you've been planning."

He threw his head back and laughed.

"Shush you. I was going to ask you something. Stop getting me hard." He looked down at his cock. "Or *harder*."

Shea snorted then sat up, her breasts jiggling when she did so.

He loved how she jiggled.

"What's up?"

He cupped her face, his heart racing. He took a deep breath and took the plunge. "I want to be with you forever, Shea. Forever. Marry me. Have lots of babies with me. Just *be* with me."

Shea's eyes widened, and she threw her arms around his neck, pressing her lips to his. Shep scrambled and pulled her closer.

He pulled back. "Is that a yes? I know we've only been seeing each other a few months but..."

"Shut up. Of course it's a yes!"

Shep smiled, joy filling him. "Fuck yeah. You're mine, soon to be Mrs. Montgomery."

Shea licked her lips. "Shea Montgomery? I love it."

"Not as much as I love you."

She ran a hand through his hair. "I love it when you get sappy, my sexy, tattooed, bearded man."

He leaned down and ran his scruff over her cheek. "Only for you, Shea. Only for you."

Shea had given him everything.

His future.

His happiness.

His inspiration.

Now he had a lifetime to pay her back.

Coming Next in the Montgomery Ink Series:

Sassy gets her story in a special bonus prequel, INK REUNITED

The first full length novel, Montgomery Ink Book 1, features Austin: DELICATE INK

A Note from Carrie Ann

Thank you so much for reading **INK INSPIRED**. I do hope if you liked this story, that you would please leave a review. Not only does a review spread the word to other readers, they let us authors know if you'd like to see more stories like this from us. I love hearing from readers and talking to them when I can. If you want to make sure you know what's coming next from me, you can sign up for my newsletter at www.CarrieAnnRyan.com; follow me on twitter at @CarrieAnnRyan, or like my Facebook page. I also have a Facebook Fan Club where we have trivia, chats, and other goodies. You guys are the reason I get to do what I do and I thank you.

Make sure you're signed up for my MAILING LIST so you can know when the next releases are available as well as find giveaways and FREE READS.

The Montgomery Ink series is an on going series. I hope you get a chance to catch up!

Montgomery Ink:
Book 0.5: Ink Inspired
Book 0.6: Ink Reunited
Book 1: Delicate Ink
Book 1.5 Forever Ink
Book 2: Tempting Boundaries
Book 3: Harder than Words
Book 4: Written in Ink (Coming Oct 2015)

Want to keep up to date with the next Carrie Ann Ryan Release? Receive Text Alerts easily!
Text CARRIE to 24587

About Carrie Ann and her Books

New York Times and USA Today Bestselling Author Carrie Ann Ryan never thought she'd be a writer. Not really. No, she loved math and science and even went on to graduate school in chemistry. Yes, she read as a kid and devoured teen fiction and Harry Potter, but it wasn't until someone handed her a romance book in her late teens that she realized that there was something out there just for her. When another author suggested she use the voices in her head for good and not evil, The Redwood Pack and all her other stories were born.

Carrie Ann is a bestselling author of over twenty novels and novellas and has so much more on her mind (and on her spreadsheets *grins*) that she isn't planning on giving up her dream anytime soon.

www.CarrieAnnRyan.com

Redwood Pack Series:
Book 1: An Alpha's Path
Book 2: A Taste for a Mate
Book 3: Trinity Bound
Book 3.5: A Night Away
Book 4: Enforcer's Redemption
Book 4.5: Blurred Expectations
Book 4.7: Forgiveness
Book 5: Shattered Emotions
Book 6: Hidden Destiny
Book 6.5: A Beta's Haven
Book 7: Fighting Fate
Book 7.5 Loving the Omega
Book 7.7: The Hunted Heart
Book 8: Wicked Wolf

The Talon Pack (Following the Redwood Pack Series):

Book 1: Tattered Loyalties
Book 2: An Alpha's Choice
Book 3: Mated in Mist (Coming in 2016)

The Redwood Pack Volumes:
Redwood Pack Vol 1
Redwood Pack Vol 2
Redwood Pack Vol 3
Redwood Pack Vol 4
Redwood Pack Vol 5
Redwood Pack Vol 6

Montgomery Ink:
Book 0.5: Ink Inspired
Book 0.6: Ink Reunited
Book 1: Delicate Ink
Book 1.5 Forever Ink
Book 2: Tempting Boundaries
Book 3: Harder than Words
Book 4: Written in Ink (Coming Oct 2015)

The Branded Pack Series:
(Written with Alexandra Ivy)
Books 1 & 2: Stolen and Forgiven

Books 3 & 4: Abandoned and Unseen (Coming Sept 2015)

Dante's Circle Series:
Book 1: Dust of My Wings
Book 2: Her Warriors' Three Wishes
Book 3: An Unlucky Moon
The Dante's Circle Box Set (Contains Books 1-3)
Book 3.5: His Choice
Book 4: Tangled Innocence
Book 5: Fierce Enchantment
Book 6: An Immortal's Song (Coming in 2016)

Holiday, Montana Series:
Book 1: Charmed Spirits
Book 2: Santa's Executive
Book 3: Finding Abigail
The Holiday Montana Box Set (Contains Books 1-3)
Book 4: Her Lucky Love
Book 5: Dreams of Ivory

Tempting Signs Series:
Finally Found You

Excerpt: Wicked Wolf

From New York Times Bestselling Author Carrie Ann Ryan's Redwood Pack Series

There were times to drool over a sexy wolf.

Sitting in the middle of a war room disguised as a board meeting was not one of those times.

Gina Jamenson did her best not to stare at the dark-haired, dark-eyed man across the room. The hint of ink peeking out from under his shirt made her want to pant. She *loved* ink and this wolf clearly had a lot of it. Her own wolf within nudged at her, a soft brush beneath her skin, but she ignored her. When her wolf whimpered, Gina promised herself that she'd go on a long run in the forest later. She didn't understand why her wolf was acting like this, but she'd deal with it when she was in a better place. She just couldn't let her wolf have control right then—even for a man such as the gorgeous specimen a mere ten feet from her.

Today was more important than the wants and feelings of a half wolf, half witch hybrid.

Today was the start of a new beginning.

At least that's what her dad had told her.

Considering her father was also the Alpha of the Redwood Pack, he would be in the know. She'd been adopted into the family when she'd been a young girl. A rogue wolf during the war had killed her parents, setting off a long line of events that had changed her life.

As it was, Gina wasn't quite sure how she'd ended up in the meeting between the two Packs, the Redwoods and the Talons. Sure, the Packs had met before over the past fifteen years of their treaty, but this meeting seemed different.

This one seemed more important somehow.

And they'd invited—more like *demanded*—Gina to attend.

At twenty-six, she knew she was the youngest wolf in the room by far. Most of the wolves were around her father's age, somewhere in the hundreds. The dark-eyed wolf might have been slightly younger than that, but only slightly if the power radiating off of him was any indication.

Wolves lived a long, long time. She'd heard stories of her

people living into their thousands, but she'd never met any of the wolves who had. The oldest wolf she'd met was a friend of the family, Emeline, who was over five hundred. That number boggled her mind even though she'd grown up knowing the things that went bump in the night were real.

Actually, she *was* one of the things that went bump in the night.

"Are we ready to begin?" Gideon, the Talon Alpha, asked, his voice low. It held that dangerous edge that spoke of power and authority.

Her wolf didn't react the way most wolves would, head and eyes down, shoulders dropped. Maybe if she'd been a weaker wolf, she'd have bowed to his power, but as it was, her wolf was firmly entrenched within the Redwoods. Plus, it wasn't as if

Gideon was *trying* to make her bow just then. No, those words had simply been spoken in his own voice.

Commanding without even trying.

Then again, he *was* an Alpha.

Kade, her father, looked around the room at each of his wolves and nodded. "Yes. It is time."

Their formality intrigued her. Yes, they were two Alphas who held a treaty and worked together in times of war, but she had thought they were also friends.

Maybe today was even more important than she'd realized.

Gideon released a sigh that spoke of years of angst and worries. She didn't know the history of the Talons as well as she probably should have, so she didn't know exactly why there was always an air of sadness and pain around the Alpha.

Maybe after this meeting, she'd be able to find out more.

Of course, in doing so, she'd have to *not* look at a certain wolf in the corner. His gaze was so intense she was sure he was studying her. She felt it down in her bones, like a fiery caress that promised something more.

Or maybe she was just going crazy and needed to find a wolf to scratch the itch.

She might not be looking for a mate, but she wouldn't say no to something else. Wolves were tactile creatures after all.

"Gina?"

She blinked at the sound of Kade's voice and turned to him.

She was the only one standing other than the two wolves in charge of security—her uncle Adam, the Enforcer, and the dark-eyed wolf.

Well, *that* was embarrassing.

She kept her head down and forced herself not to blush. From the heat on her neck, she was pretty sure she'd failed in the latter.

"Sorry," she mumbled then sat down next to another uncle, Jasper, the Beta of the Pack.

Although the Alphas had called this meeting, she wasn't sure what it would entail. Each Alpha had come with their Beta, a wolf in charge of security...and her father had decided to bring her.

Her being there didn't make much sense in the grand scheme of things since it put the power on the Redwoods' side, but she wasn't about to question authority in front of another Pack. That at least had been ingrained in her training.

"Let's get started then," Kade said after he gave her a nod. "Gideon? Do you want to begin?"

Gina held back a frown. They *were* acting more formal than usual, so that hadn't been her imagination. The Talons and the Redwoods had formed a treaty during the latter days of the war between the Redwoods and the Centrals. It wasn't as though these were two newly acquainted Alphas meeting for the first time. Though maybe when it came to Pack matters, Alphas couldn't truly be friends.

What a lonely way to live.

"It's been fifteen years since the end of the Central War, yet there hasn't been a single mating between the two Packs," Gideon said, shocking her.

Gina blinked. Really? That couldn't be right. She was sure there had to have been *some* cross-Pack mating.

Right?

"That means that regardless of the treaties we signed, we don't believe the moon goddess has seen fit to fully accept us as a unit," Kade put in.

"What do you mean?" she asked, then shut her mouth. She was the youngest wolf here and wasn't formally titled or ranked. She should *not* be speaking right now.

She felt the gaze of the dark-eyed wolf on her, but she didn't turn to look. Instead, she kept her head down in a show of respect to the Alphas.

"You can ask questions, Gina. It's okay," Kade said, the tone of his voice not changing, but, as his daughter, she heard the softer edge. "And what I mean is, mating comes from the moon goddess. Yes, we can find our own versions of mates by not bonding fully, but a true bond, a true potential mate, is chosen by the moon goddess. That's how it's always been in the past."

Gideon nodded. "There haven't been many matings within the Talons in general."

Gina sucked in a breath, and the Beta of the Talons, Mitchell, turned her way. "Yes," Mitchell said softly. "It's that bad. It could be that in this period of change within our own pack hierarchy, our members just haven't found mates yet, but that doesn't seem likely. There's something else going on."

Gina knew Gideon—as well as the rest of his brothers and cousins—had come into power at some point throughout the end of the Central War during a period of the Talon's own unrest, but she didn't know the full history. She wasn't even sure Kade or the rest of the Pack royalty did.

There were some things that were intensely private within a Pack that could not—and should not—be shared.

Jasper tapped his fingers along the table. As the Redwood Beta, it was his job to care for their needs and recognize hidden threats that the Enforcer and Alpha might not see. The fact that he was here told Gina that the Pack could be in trouble from something *within* the Pack, rather than an outside force that Adam, the Enforcer, would be able to see through his own bonds and power.

"Since Finn became the Heir to the Pack at such a young age, it has changed a few things on our side," Jasper said softly. Finn was her brother, Melanie and Kade's oldest biological child. "The younger generation will be gaining their powers and bonds to the goddess earlier than would otherwise be expected." Her uncle looked at her, and she kept silent. "That means the current Pack leaders will one day not have the bonds we have to our Pack now. But like most healthy Packs, that doesn't mean we're set aside. It only means we will be there to aid the new hierarchy while they learn their powers. That's how it's always been in our Pack, and in others, but it's been a very long time since it's happened to us."

"Gina will one day be the Enforcer," Adam said from behind her. "I don't know when, but it will be soon. The other kids aren't old enough yet to tell who will take on which role, but since Gina is in her twenties, the shifts are happening."

The room grew silent, with an odd sense of change settling over her skin like an electric blanket turned on too high.

She didn't speak. She'd known about her path, had dreamed the dreams from the moon goddess herself. But that didn't mean she wanted the

Talons to know all of this. It seemed...private somehow.

"What does this have to do with mating?" she asked, wanting to focus on something else.

Gideon gave her a look, and she lowered her eyes. He might not be her Alpha, but he was still a dominant wolf. Yes, she hadn't lowered her eyes before, but she'd been rocked a bit since Adam had told the others of her future. She didn't want to antagonize anyone when Gideon clearly wanted to show his power. Previously, everything had been casual; now it clearly was not.

Kade growled beside her. "Gideon."

The Talon Alpha snorted, not smiling, but moved his gaze. "It's fun to see how she reacts."

"She's my daughter and the future Enforcer."

"*She* is right here, so how about you answer my question?"

Jasper chuckled by her side, and Gina wondered how quickly she could reach the nearest window and jump. It couldn't be that far. She wouldn't die from the fall or anything, and she'd be able to run home.

Quickly.

"Mating," Kade put in, the laughter in his eyes fading, "is only a small part of the problem. When we sent Caym back to hell with the other demons, it changed the power structure within the Packs as well as outside them. The Centrals who fought against us died because they'd lost their souls to the demon. The Centrals that had hidden from the old Alphas ended up being lone wolves. They're not truly a Pack yet because the goddess hasn't made anyone an Alpha."

"Then you have the Redwoods, with a hierarchy shift

within the younger generation," Gideon said. "And the Talons' new power dynamic is only fifteen years old, and we haven't had a mating in long enough that it's starting to worry us."

"Not that you'd say that to the rest of the Pack," Mitchell mumbled.

"It's best they don't know," Gideon said, the sounds of an old argument telling Gina there was more going on here than what they revealed.

Interesting.

"There aren't any matings between our two Packs, and I know the trust isn't fully there," Kade put in then sighed. "I don't know how to fix that myself. I don't think I can."

"You're the Alpha," Jasper said calmly. "If you *tell* them to get along with the other wolves, they will, and for the most part, they have. But it isn't as authentic as if they find that trust on their own. We've let them go this long on their own, but now, I think we need to find another way to have our Packs more entwined."

The dark-eyed wolf came forward then. "You've seen something," he growled.

Dear goddess. His voice.

Her wolf perked, and she shoved her down. This wasn't the time.

"We've seen...something, Quinn," Kade answered.

Quinn. That was his name.

Sexy.

And again, *so* not the time.

Tattered Loyalties

From New York Times Bestselling Author Carrie Ann Ryan's Talon Pack Series

When the great war between the Redwoods and the Centrals occurred three decades ago, the Talon Pack risked their lives for the side of good. After tragedy struck, Gideon Brentwood became the Alpha of the Talons. But the Pack's stability is threatened, and he's forced to take mate—only the one fate puts in his path is the woman he shouldn't want.

Though the daughter of the Redwood Pack's Beta, Brie Jamenson has known peace for most of her life. When she finds the man who could be her mate, she's shocked to discover Gideon is the Alpha wolf of the Talon Pack. As a submissive, her strength lies in her heart, not her claws. But if her new Pack disagrees or disapproves, the consequences could be fatal.

As the worlds Brie and Gideon have always known begin to shift, they must face their challenges together in order to help their Pack and seal their bond. But when the Pack is threatened from the inside, Gideon doesn't know who he can trust and Brie's life could be forfeit in the crossfire. It will take the strength of an Alpha and the courage of his mate to realize where true loyalties lie.

Delicate Ink

From New York Times Bestselling Author Carrie Ann Ryan's Montgomery Ink Series

On the wrong side of thirty, Austin Montgomery is ready to settle down. Unfortunately, his inked sleeves and scruffy beard isn't the suave business appearance some women crave. Only finding a woman who can deal with his job, as a tattoo artist and owner of Montgomery Ink, his seven meddling siblings, and his own gruff attitude won't be easy.

Finding a man is the last thing on Sierra Elder's mind. A recent transplant to Denver, her focus is on opening her own boutique. Wanting to cover up scars that run deeper than her flesh, she finds in Austin a man that truly gets to her—in more ways than one.

Although wary, they embark on a slow, tempestuous burn of a relationship. When blasts from both their pasts intrude on their present, however, it will take more than a promise of what could be to keep them together.

Dust of My Wings

From New York Times Bestselling Author Carrie Ann Ryan's Dante's Circle Series

Humans aren't as alone as they choose to believe. Every human possesses a trait of supernatural that lays dormant within their genetic make-up. Centuries of diluting and breeding have allowed humans to think they are alone and untouched by magic. But what happens when something changes?

Neat freak lab tech, Lily Banner lives her life as any ordinary human. She's dedicated to her work and loves to hang out with her friends at Dante's Circle, their local bar. When she discovers a strange blue dust at work she meets a handsome stranger holding secrets – and maybe her heart. But after a close call with a thunderstorm, she may not be as ordinary as she thinks.

Shade Griffin is a warrior angel sent to Earth to protect the supernaturals' secrets. One problem, he can't stop leaving dust in odd places around town. Now he has to find every ounce of his dust and keep the presence of the supernatural a secret. But after a close encounter with a sexy lab tech and a lightning quick connection, his millennia old loyalties may shift and he could lose more than just his wings in the chaos.

Warning: Contains a sexy angel with a choice to make and a green-eyed lab tech who dreams of a dark-winged stranger. Oh yeah, and a shocking spark that's sure to leave them begging for more.